KNAVE OF DIAMONDS

Sharon is employed by a retailer to write some PR text about Patrick, a famous jewellery designer, who's creating an exclusive collection for the everyday woman. Patrick's initial resentment of Sharon changes when he gets to know her, whilst she admits that he's a fascinating man. If only other women didn't think so too! Then as Sharon and Patrick visit Hong Kong for a photo session things begin to buzz — only to fall apart. What has fate designed for them?

WENDY KREMER

KNAVE OF DIAMONDS

Complete and Unabridged

LINFORD
Leicester

First published in Great Britain in 2010

First Linford Edition
published 2011

British Library CIP Data

Kremer, Wendy.
  Knave of diamonds. - -
  (Linford romance library)
  1. Love stories.
  2. Large type books.
  I. Title II. Series
  823.9'2–dc22

  ISBN 978–1–4448–0633–5

Published by
F. A. Thorpe (Publishing)
Anstey, Leicestershire

Set by Words & Graphics Ltd.
Anstey, Leicestershire
Printed and bound in Great Britain by
T. J. International Ltd., Padstow, Cornwall

1

Standing centre stage, the owner of the exclusive jewellery shop was about to introduce Patrick Caine to the throng, all of whom had received personal invitations to attend the presentation of his newest collection.

Early October winds had buffeted her along, but Sharon Robinson didn't mind braving the elements this morning; she'd been sent by her employers, the local newspaper, to cover the event. It wasn't every day that a well-known personality visited the small town. A number of wealthy commuters lived locally now, and these days the traditional jewellers in the High Street catered to a more exclusive clientele — one where money was no object. Sharon speculated on where local young couples went to get their engagement rings nowadays. They wouldn't be able to afford any of the

1

ones on display here today.

Sharon was pleased to be covering something unusual for a change. Her reporting skills were usually restricted to monotonous local happenings. A personal appearance by someone like Patrick Caine brought fresh wind into her job for a while. Sharon had been watching him for a couple of minutes, and stored impressions as she did so. He towered over the other men standing near him by several inches and he had a swarthy skin and brown, almost black, hair. In particular, she noticed his hands; they were beautiful, long-fingered and strong. There was a restless energy in his movements and his dark but greying hair gave him a distinguished appearance.

Patrick stood waiting, his eyes casually skimming the crowd, not expecting to see anything to excite his interest. Scanning the room, he took in Sharon's wide eyes, supple young body, high cheekbones and her resolutely set mouth. His black-clad figure stiffened and he lost a half-second of his life. He clenched his mouth tighter and threw her a meaningful look. Sharon noticed and wondered why she'd aroused censure in the eyes of someone she'd never seen before. He looked at her intently with cold dark grey eyes and turned to murmur something to the man on his right. The man, with a wide-shouldered, rangy body, and touches of humour around his eyes, looked at her and then drifted away into the jostle of people standing near Patrick Caine. Sharon arrested her wandering thoughts and began to store some details of the event in her mind before it was all over.

The owner of the shop called for silence and opened the proceedings. 'I'm sure that most of you are familiar with the work and career of Patrick Caine and he needs no detailed introduction from me. Mr Caine is one of today's foremost jewellery designers, and his field of activity has recently widened to designing and creating costume jewellery for opera.

'No doubt, some of you have read about the highly acclaimed, breath-taking and elaborate pieces he created for a recent performance of Aida at the Metropolitan Opera House in New York. Mr Caine comes from near London. His father is the well-known sculptor Leon Caine so it's likely that he had a generous share of artistic genes from the moment he was born. His present collection, you can admire some of it here today, is a striking and original one. The pieces are all unique and outstanding, each one in its own very special way. All of the jewellery carries his hallmark — simplicity of design, luxurious materials, and subtle decadence. I'd like to introduce Mr Caine now, and hope that he can give us some insight into some of the ideas that motivated and stimulated him to produce the beautiful items you can see today. Ladies and gentlemen, Patrick Caine!'

Patrick acknowledged the applause with a slight nod of his head. His voice was crisp and clear. 'Thank you for your introduction, Mr Russell and thank you for coming this morning, ladies and gentlemen. I'm sure you appreciate that weeks and even months lie between the design and its finished form when the pieces of jewellery go on show, like today. It would take too long to explain each item's progress in detail, but I hope you like the pieces I've brought, and if you need more details or information, my partner Andrew Bryce or I will be pleased to help. To be honest, sometimes I'm loathe to part with many of the pieces, because each one is part of me and my life, but in the end, good sense usually wins the upper hand because I have to make a living! I'm always delighted to see my work being worn by people who like my jewellery as much as I do myself! Apart from aesthetic reasons, it soothes my bank manager's nerves no end.' There was a soft ripple of laughter. 'Jewellery should underline the individuality and character of its wearer, and primarily give immense pleasure. Enjoy viewing the collection; I hope it will encourage you to buy something.'

There was another round of applause, and the crowd began to circulate. Patrick Caine was soon surrounded by people.

Sharon noted the touch of humour in his address, so he wasn't wholly the dour character she assumed him to be. There was still an air of isolation about his figure, even in a crowded room like this. She'd have to search the internet for some personal information; he didn't look like someone she could approach personally. She scrabbled around in her large shoulder bag for a notebook to jot down some of his speech to quote in her article.

'Hi there!' Sharon looked up and was startled to find Patrick Caine's partner holding out his hand. 'Andrew Bryce, and you are?'

She took his hand briefly. 'Sharon Robinson.' She smiled at him.

Her facial bones were delicately

carved and her smooth skin glowed with pale gold undertones. He could tell, straight away, why Patrick had noticed her. He said smoothly, with no discernable change of expression. 'Are you a jewellery fan; a buyer?' Someone passed with a tray of champagne. He lifted two glasses and handed her one.

There was a trace of laughter in Sharon's voice. She took a sip of the bubbling liquid and answered. 'No! I could never afford to buy anything on display here. I don't know anything about jewellery either. I represent the local press. The visit of a well-known personality is rare in this part of the world so I've been instructed to write a 300 word article about Mr Caine. He just mentioned you're his partner?'

The young man nodded. His immediate reaction was relief that she was only a local reporter, and her reason for being here was quite logical. She was clearly unaware of any resemblance and wasn't out to exploit the situation at all. 'I see! We always welcome some extra publicity.' He looked around. 'It's quite a good turnout this morning, for a small town like this!'

'Yes! I suspect most of the people here are new to the community. Up until a few years ago, it was a quiet market town. Then commuters from London discovered it was easy to travel to London from here, and that made it an attractive neighbourhood for them. The result being that house prices have soared and local shops cater for an entirely new kind of clientele these days.'

'Do you come from around here?'

'Yes, I do. I grew up not far away and I now live on the edge of the town.'

'And do you mind — about the changes?'

She shrugged. 'I guess it's like everything else in life; you have to take the good with the bad. I think it's a shame that young people who were born locally are now being pushed out of the market if they want to buy their own home, but on the other end of the scale there are others making a bomb in selling off vacant cottages and houses.'

Patrick Caine came through a gap towards them. 'Andy, Russell told me someone is haggling about the price of that needle pendant with the sapphires. Will you handle it? Don't go down in price, there's too much platinum and gold in it — not to mention the amount of work I put into it. Oh — and there's someone over there who wants more information about the weight content of the gold and platinum bracelet. Do you have the list?'

Andrew Bryce nodded. 'Okay! Who's after the pendant?'

His dark brows lifted. 'That couple standing under that wall clock, over there — the woman in a lilac dress, with flamboyant snake earrings.'

Andrew nodded briefly to Sharon, and sauntered off towards the couple.

He had classically handsome features, and a muscle clenched along his jaw as he viewed her. Sharon grabbed her chance. 'Mr Caine, could you give me a few minutes of your time later, for a short interview for the local news-paper?'

His dark grey eyes surveyed her; they were like bits of stone. 'I don't give interviews.' He gave her a brief nod and walked briefly away.

What a disagreeable man! Her wealth of dark hair shook as she straightened her shoulders. She'd need to be careful when she wrote her article not to let her antagonism flow into it. She wandered through the room studying various pieces, picked up some glossy bro-chures, and noted the extravagant prices. Andrew Bryce was busy and didn't attempt to join her again, but he lifted his hand and sent her a good humoured smile as he noticed she was on her way out.

★ ★ ★

Rain clouds were gathering and leaves lay around in wet drifts. Colder weather was replacing a spell of mild days they'd had recently — perhaps the last this year. Winter was finally on the way. When she reached the office, in a backwater street overlooking the river, her editor asked her how it had gone. She mumbled something undistinguishable, gave a thumbs-down sign, and headed towards her desk in the corner. She had to go to the local court later on, to report on a case of breaking and entering they'd covered in the newspaper. Sharon decided to use the spare time to gather some information for her article on Patrick Caine. She hoped the jeweller had employed a photographer. A picture would pep up her article no end.

Searching the internet, she found several items of interest about Patrick Caine. He lived in London, had a flat in Hong Kong, and another in Paris. He was a widower and, at present, it was rumoured that he was escorting Blair Darleen, a renowned soprano. His wife had been killed in a skiing accident six years ago, and she'd been the youngest daughter of Lord Lofthouse. Sharon searched for pictures, and the only one she found straight off was a small one of Patrick and his wife against the background of the Rocky Mountains. She was smartly elegant in a figure hugging white ski-suit. Her face was in a ski cap, and her eyes were hidden behind large sunglasses. Patrick Caine was very recognisable; he stood there looking handsome and at ease, with a commanding air of self-confidence. There were lots of particulars about his education, his training and lists of the various prizes and awards that he'd won over the last couple of years.

Sharon decided to write a very neutral and unbiased article. Thinking about his manner and abrupt departure when she asked for an interview this morning, she decided if he ever read the article, he might be the kind of personality who might split hairs about every single word that he didn't like. Sharon didn't want to cause any trouble for her paper, or her boss. Mr Caine probably wouldn't ever see the article, but to be on the safe side she'd write an informative article and leave out most of the personal bits.

★   ★   ★

Patrick was clad in jeans and a faded blue work shirt. Sunlight spilled through the windows of the small atelier on to the benches where some of the tools of his trade were scattered. He sat on a revolving stool in the half-circular cut-out workbench, where he was employed on creating his latest design. His thick dark hair tapered neatly to his collar. He ran his long fingers through it, then rested his hands on his thigh and looked up at his partner. His brows drew together in an angry frown and his eyes were looking into the past.

The silence lengthened until he said, 'I don't have to tell you that I don't like the idea one bit! You saw the likeness to Jessica yourself. Do you imagine I'd enjoy having this woman trailing us for days or weeks?'

His friend made a calming gesture with his hand. 'I thought you'd say that — but it was your idea to bring out a collection for the woman on the street, and it was your idea to agree to the contract with this chain store! They have rights now, and we can't send them off with a flea in their ears unless we have a pretty good excuse.'

He moved towards the coffee machine and helped himself. 'Apparently, one of the T&M company directors was at that jeweller's shop we visited a few weeks ago, and he read the report about it later in the local rag. He was impressed by the text, and thought the writer would be ideal to produce copy for the PR campaign launching the collection in December. Apparently his word carries weight!'

Patrick's expression was clouded in anger and a hard edge crept into his voice. 'And so I'm forced to continually confront some strange woman, who reminds me constantly of my dead wife? Haven't I at least some kind of choice in the matter?'

Andrew looked uncomfortable; he shrugged his shoulders. 'The article was well-written Patrick, I've brought you a copy.' He took a newspaper cutting out of his wallet and put it on the bench. Patrick Caine ignored it. 'She can write prose like Shakespeare for all I care.'

Andrew met his eyes and looked resigned. 'Jessica has been dead six years, Patrick. Six years! This woman can't help it if she resembles her. The likeness isn't as strong as you think; it's just the first impression. You didn't give her more than a cursory glance; I did.' He paused, knowing what a sensitive area it was. 'You've moved on; you've had several girlfriends over the last couple of years. Why does a fluke like this bother you so much? She'd be there to do a job, nothing more!'

Patrick crossed his arms. 'If you don't understand, there's no point in me trying to explain is there? Seeing that woman brought back the memories. To some extent, I was responsible for

Jessica's death. I let her take that ski-slope, even though I knew it would test her abilities to the limit.'

'That's complete nonsense, and you know it.' Andrew lifted his hand to silence him. 'Jessica was always after a new challenge, looking for a fresh kick! I can afford to be honest with you, because I'm your friend. Jessica enjoyed provoking you, and she wanted to bring out your protective instincts by doing things that were way beyond her capabilities. She was determined to go down that ski-slope, even though you warned her it was too difficult. When she lost control and ran straight into a tree, it was entirely her own fault, not yours. You couldn't have stopped her once she'd made up her mind; so it's about time you shook off this complex of guilt you have about what happened!'

Patrick stared at him, but didn't answer. He turned away and clenched the edge of the bench. 'I still don't like this woman barging in on my life.'

Andrew replied quietly. 'She isn't barging in! The chain store wants her. As far as I gather, she needed lots of persuasion before she said she'd even consider it.' He put the mug back on the tray. 'Think about it. If you honestly can't come to terms with having her around for a couple of weeks, let me know. I'll get us out of the contract somehow, but it will mean the collection will die a sudden death, you might be asked to pay some compensation, and I doubt if any similar kind of commission will be offered to you again in the future.' He moved towards the door. 'See you later!'

Patrick stared out of the window. He knew deep down he was acting illogically but this strange woman had stirred up all the memories again. Patrick also knew that his marriage was in deep trouble long before the accident happened. It hadn't been just sugar and spice to live with Jessica. Her mother died when she was small and her father had always pandered to her every wish;

17

she was headstrong, obstinate and completely spoiled. After their whirl-wind courtship, he continued to pander and indulge her, because that was what made her happy. He loved beautiful things and Jessica was beautiful; huge amethyst eyes, dainty features, and a slim wild beauty. She was also unpredictable and volatile, and she enjoyed things that Patrick didn't — parties, painting the town red, and continual socialising. Arguments had started to govern their relationship long before she died. His glance caught the newspaper-cutting on the table. He picked it up and read it.

* ★ ★

Sharon faced Andrew across a bistro table in a cafe near to the T&M's company headquarters where she'd just been for an interview. Sharon learned he was a lawyer, and he handled Patrick's legal and business affairs. The company representatives had explained

18

what they judged Sharon's part in the deal would be. They'd given her 48 hours to decide.

After the meeting, she and Andrew had walked back to the lift together and he'd suggested a cup of coffee. Andrew was glad to have a chance to tell Sharon about Jessica.

She picked up her cappuccino with its thick layer of froth and took a sip. She nodded. 'I see; what a fluke! Do we really look alike? I just thought he was merely disagreeable by nature. I presume a lot of artists can be temperamental and egoistical.'

Andrew gave her a weak answering smile and studied her quiet oval face. Her hair was black, straight and short, and cut closely to the shape of her head. She had a gentle beauty and something Andrew defined as presence. Jessica had hungered for the limelight; this girl didn't need that kind of attention, you'd always remember her for her character and personality. Intelligence and understanding flickered in her eyes and he tried to be honest. 'There is a fleeting similarity, but speaking personally, it fades very quickly, because you have a completely different temperament.'

'No two people are totally alike! Even twins.' She looked down and said calmly. 'If T&M hadn't offered such a lot of money, I don't think I'd consider for a moment, but it's a real temptation. My biggest problem is that I'm sure my boss won't keep my old job open although T&M have made vague promises to help find me another job afterwards.'

He nodded understandingly. 'Why don't you force their hand a little, and get it written into the contract? Tell them that it's the only thing holding you back, and I'll tell them Patrick insists on you and no one else.'

She regarded him with a speculative gaze. 'Do you think that if I keep out of his way as much as possible, that it would work? I'm being paid to observe and describe what I see, but I can't if I'm shoved into a far corner all the time. Now that I understand about why he felt annoyed, I'll try not to be a pain in the neck, and do my job, I do need access to him and what he does.'

His smile relaxed measurably. 'I can tell you have bags of perception and understanding; that will help him and you no end. I'll try to act as a buffer if necessary, whenever I can. I'm sure Patrick will soon get used to you.'

Sharon had her doubts. Patrick Caine was a complicated, artistic man. She'd never dealt with anyone quite like him before. The job attracted her very much — a completely new kind of challenge. Producing pertinent text about where he went and what he did for a couple of weeks wouldn't be too difficult and she'd enjoy it. Was it worth facing his constant hostility?

2

A month later, she was figuring how not to intrude into Patrick Caine's life, or get in his way, and still do her job. Andrew provided her with a rough idea of what was on his agenda in the coming weeks and Sharon decided she'd make the most of her opportunities from the word go, in case her stay was short-lived. She wondered why T&M hadn't used one of their own PR people — but perhaps they were good at producing advertising text after someone else provided the basic ideas. She theorised that the job might only last a couple of days if Patrick Caine rejected her presence outright — but the contract promised her a job in town when the contract finished so she wasn't going to worry about that possibility now. T&M had provided her with a one-room flat for the duration and generous travelling expenses so she'd relax — and concentrate on feeding them with copy for their campaign.

The first time she acted as observer, it was at a meeting between Patrick and the owners of a small jewellery shop in a Kensington arcade. Angry grey clouds were hurrying across the sky. She was wearing her smartest coat — her smartest, not her warmest. She pulled her scarf tighter around her neck to keep out the cold and shoved her gloved hands deeper in her pockets. Piles of ankle-deep red and gold leaves covered the ground on the opposite pavement. Andrew and Patrick turned up at the appointed time. Andrew smiled; Patrick looked at her and managed a curt nod, before he continued on towards the covered passageway.

Andrew supplied her with the information. 'Hi there! This place is fairly exclusive; they've been buying Patrick's stuff practically from the very beginning.' He added quietly. 'I don't normally accompany him everywhere, but I thought it might help ease you into the situation if I came along today.'

Sharon was grateful and said so.

She followed them inside. A middle-aged couple, clearly the owners, greeted Patrick warmly. Andrew introduced her as a junior-assistant. There were no customers waiting, so they all went into a small room behind the sales area. The conversation drifted; there was talk about mutual memories of past deals and information about who'd bought his last pieces. Patrick opened a small leather case he was carrying, spread a large square of black velvet on the desk and selected some pieces of jewellery from the pull-out drawers. The middle-aged couple considered, examined, discussed, and finally picked out several pieces they liked. Prices were noted, a bit of haggling went on, but everyone seemed satisfied in the end.

The owner looked at his watch. 'What about lunch Patrick? We've already booked a table at Chez Louis.'

For the first time, Sharon saw him

smile. She was astounded by the difference it made.

'With pleasure; the best fish restaurant in London!'

The couple nodded, clearly pleased. They collected their coats, gave instructions to a young man behind the counter in the shop on their way, and led the way out. The dark angry clouds were still scudding across the sky. Sharon nodded to Andrew and the shop owners, and moved away.

The shop owner looked at her and said. 'Young lady, you're included too, of course.'

The colour rose in her cheeks. 'That's very kind of you, but I have another appointment. I hope you enjoy your lunch. Goodbye!' She walked determinedly across to the bus stop on the other side of the road and stood waiting in the blustery winds, the leaves dancing at her feet. She hadn't spoken one word to Patrick or he to her, but she had gained an impression of how he handled customers, and how they reacted to him. She'd get it down on paper before the impressions faded. She had a job to do, and she was going to do it to the best of her ability, with or without his blessing.

★ ★ ★

A day later, she phoned to ask Andrew if she could watch Patrick working. It would help her if she could see a little of the creative process. Sharon wondered if persuasion was necessary, but she decided not to worry; she didn't want to get annoyed. The situation was not her fault. Andrew phoned back and gave her a day and time when she could call.

Patrick opened the door with a flourish. He stood straight and tall; his square jaw tensed visibly when he saw her standing on the top step. She took her hands out her figure-flattering red wool jacket and tried a smile, but it didn't work on him. He didn't respond.

'Morning, Mr Caine! I hope you

won't mind me watching you for a while? I'd like a better idea of what's behind your working day. Andrew said it was alright for me to call?'

He nodded perfunctorily. His grey eyes were flat and as unreadable as stone. Any woman would be attracted by his striking features and sensual appeal and Sharon wasn't immune, but his attitude significantly dampened any personal interest she had. He turned away without a word. She followed him and shut the door. As she tagged along through the house to his studio on the far side of the building, she saw that his home suited his image — but had she expected anything else? From without, and within, the house was a split-level architectural fulfilment. The interior had white walls, grey slate floors, wooden fittings of teak, narrow windows of smoked glass, and the furniture was leather and chrome. Placed strategically in front of the sitting room window, and overlooking the sunlit garden, was a large abstract form in polished black stone. Sharon mused that it was probably one of his father's creations; it looked good.

Once they entered what was clearly his studio, Sharon decided to try to set things right. 'Mr Caine, I understand why you find my presence disconcerting, but I'll try not to get in your way. I don't want to upset you. The resemblance to your wife is not my fault! I am only trying to do a job; one that is to your advantage as well as mine.' The colour in her cheeks heightened as she faced his broad back.

He was silent and then turned. He gave her a layered look and almost ripped out the words impatiently. 'I listened to Andrew; otherwise I wouldn't have agreed to have you here. I realise opposition is counter-productive and I assume you don't intentionally want to cause problems.' Scowling, he continued. 'Good publicity is lifeblood for any creative artist. If you do your job, and leave me to do mine, we'll get along without conflict.' His eyes roamed over her figure and face, and they narrowed.

Sharon couldn't dismiss the feeling he was mentally comparing her to his dead wife, Jessica, but she didn't intend to get annoyed about something that was beyond her control. She resented his approach, but there was something about the man that made it impossible for her to completely dislike him. He was too attractive, and something about him fascinated her. She nodded. 'Good! Just tell me if I'm getting in the way!'

'You can be sure that I'll do that, Miss?'

'Robinson — Sharon Robinson.' He'd heard her name several times. Was he just feigning ignorance, or had he now decided to pay attention at last? Sharon looked around the small atelier as he settled back onto his revolving stool. The room was flooded with light from the floor to ceiling windows, but there was additional lighting where he worked. A large magnifying glass with an extending arm was fixed to one side, and he pulled it across. Sharon jumped a little, when she heard the sound of a gas burner; the hissing noise sounded like an angry serpent. He turned it up to full power and began to carefully soften a band of gold that was threaded onto what she could only describe as a kind of spindle. She watched for a while as he formed, turned, hammered, filed and polished. The muscles rippled along his broad shoulders. The room was silent, and she was too. He hadn't offered her somewhere to sit, and she had the feeling he'd almost forgotten she was there. She was tempted to get up and wander around, but she was walking on red hot coals in his company, and knew instinctively that any movement would annoy and distract him. She leaned against some cupboards and watched. After a few minutes, she fished her notebook out of her bag. The movement caught his attention and he turned to look at her.

For the first time, she saw a glimmer of amusement in his eyes as he surveyed her. He got up and went to a corner to get her a stool. 'I may be a bit of a lout, but there is no need for you to stand for the duration of your stay! Help yourself to coffee!'

She floundered and to her annoyance, her voice broke slightly when she asked. 'Would you mind if I wandered around?' In an almost friendly tone, he replied. 'No, not if it helps your writing and you don't wander in continuous circles all the time! But don't try to look over my shoulder, that makes me nervous — and I can't concentrate on my work and answer questions, so you'll have to save any for another time.'

Sharon nodded silently and he returned to his work. She sat down, made some notes, and then she helped herself quietly to coffee. The smell drifted comfortingly up to her as she circled the room with mug in hand. She studied the floor-to-ceiling display cupboards with their books and supplies. Outside the small and beautifully wild garden contained an old apple tree robbed of all its leaves by autumn's punishing winds. An inviting garden seat nearby waited patiently for the next summer. Sharon looked curiously at the unusual tools scattered on the work benches, and watched him working in complete concentration on some piece of jewellery that probably cost more than her annual wages. Sharon wondered who was taking photographs for the campaign, because this was how he ought to be presented. The creative artist completely absorbed in his work. She'd suggest that to her contact person at T&M.

She sat for a while, fascinated enough to watch as his fingers and tools perfected some emerging details. Now and then, he glanced briefly at a nearby sketch. As he'd warned her not to ask questions, she could only guess what the item would be. It could be a ring, or part of something else. When her coffee was finished, she returned the mug to the tray silently, picked up her shoulder bag and exited quietly — closing the door as softly as she could.

Patrick noticed; he paused and stared out of the window for a moment. Deep in thought, he was lost in the past for a few seconds. She seemed to be discerning. Jessica's features were fading into the past fast when he looked at Sharon's face now. The similarity ended completely when he compared their personalities. Jessica had never been very altruistic or tolerant. He turned back to his work and was glad to concentrate on the task in hand.

★ ★ ★

Sharon got into the habit of showing Andrew her texts before she submitted them to T&M. Sharon didn't want to involve Patrick directly, and she reasoned he wasn't likely to raise any objections later.

Andrew phoned her unexpectedly just as she was having breakfast.

'Patrick has some tickets for the opera this evening. Would you like to come? It would give you the chance to see him in a completely different setting — you said T&M would like some personal insights?'

Surprised and grateful Sharon said, 'That'd be great. If you're sure?'

'Covent Garden. Be in the foyer by five-thirty, it starts at six. I'll keep an eye out for you.'

'Does Patrick know that you were going to ask me?'

His voice held a touch of amusement. 'Of course! To be honest, it was my idea to invite you when he mentioned he had tickets to spare. He didn't argue or resist when I suggested you, so I think he's getting used to you.'

'Is it formal; evening dress?'

'It's not essential these days, but something swanky would be nice if you have it. Don't worry if not.'

Sharon did have something half-suitable; a figure-hugging dress, in midnight blue. She'd last worn it at a cousin's wedding. It flattered her slim figure, emphasised the blue of her eyes, and made her legs look gorgeous. She was on time, and Andrew found her easily when he arrived. She noted his admiring glance and she followed him to join Patrick Caine. Patrick and Andrew were wearing tuxedos with dress shirts and bow ties. They both looked good and, although she knew there was no room for romance, she had to admit Patrick was one of the most attractive men she'd ever seen.

She looked up at him slightly awed. 'Good evening, Mr Caine!'

He glanced at the shining hair flowing round her shoulders, the dark blue of her eyes, and the smooth unblemished skin. The colour of her dress heightened the translucence of her neck and face; her figure was curving and regal. Without much expression in his voice, he said curtly. 'I think it's time you called me Patrick, don't you? I see you more often than I do my mother! Shall we go in?' He turned, expecting the others to follow, and they did. Sharon's colour heightened and she had an urge to laugh.

She bit her lip and looked down at the carpet as she danced along in her high heels behind them. He had tickets for a box and Sharon watched from one for the first time in her life. Much to her delight, it was Madame Butterfly, and she sat entranced by the music and the performance. Patrick glanced across several times and at first he was cynical when he saw how her eyes glistened and how her breath quickened during the dramatics, but his amusement died as he noticed she was genuinely entranced by the happenings on stage. He hunched forward and concentrated on the opera and told himself there was no reason to give her any special attention.

In the interval, she said she'd remain seated. Andrew returned shortly with a glass of champagne. She accepted it gladly. 'Thank you. What luxury! I'm supposed to be here to watch Patrick, but I've been so bound up in the opera, I haven't taken a bit of notice. It's wonderful.'

He smiled understandingly. 'We're going out for a meal afterwards; Blair is coming. I hope I can persuade you to come too. Would you like to?'

Sharon didn't want to rupture the frail truce she had with Patrick by digging for personal anecdotes for T&M, but she was interested to see how Patrick and the well-known opera singer got on. Sharon decided to go — if for no other reason than just sheer female curiosity. She nodded. 'Thanks! I'd like that very much.'

Blair was just as interesting off-stage as on. She was very attractive, elegantly dressed and wore an extravagant platinum pendant with a large topaz — no doubt one of Patrick's creations. She was effervescent, charming, and also amiable and very pleasant. Sharon had expected her to be temperamental, unpredictable and difficult, but she wasn't. She had a heavenly voice and was extremely likeable into the bargain.

Sharon didn't feel Blair and Patrick had an intimate friendship; the atmosphere wasn't exciting enough for that, but perhaps they were just being discreet in public. She did notice that Patrick went to great pains to make Blair's evening enjoyable. The meal was wonderful; an Italian salad with salami and noodles, a fish dish with sharp lemon sauce, and creamed apricot with tiny balls of cantaloupe for desert. At least Patrick didn't look at Sharon with bitterness or antagonism in his eyes any more, and she was glad about that. If his trust in her stabilised, it would make her work much, much easier.

She accepted Andrew's offer to share a taxi home, and they left the other two outside the restaurant. Patrick stood for a moment and watched their taxi leave. The car dropped Sharon outside her flat, and with a friendly cheerio, Andrew continued onwards. As she was getting ready for bed, Sharon relived the evening with pleasure. She liked Andrew; he was kind, nice and uncomplicated. The opera performance had been wonderful, and she'd had an extra bonus of meeting a very charming leading soprano.

3

Next morning, dressed in sloppy jeans and an oversize T-shirt, she was enjoying her frugal breakfast at the tiny table in front of the window. Studying the newspaper, the sound of her phone cut the silence. She scrabbled through her bag to find it.

'Sharon?'

She jumped at his voice and was instantly wide awake. 'Yes.'

'I'm visiting my parents this morning. Like to come?'

The question caught her completely off-balance. She said, clearly surprised. 'Me?'

At the other end of the telephone she heard a soft chuckle. 'Yes you. You're paid to trail me all over the place aren't you? I thought you'd like some family stuff?'

Her throat was dry. She only

hesitated for a moment. Why shouldn't she be honest with him? 'I'm surprised that you offer. In fact I'm amazed.'

There was a rustling and a pause at the other end of the line. 'I've come to realise that it's better for someone I know to write objective articles, than to let someone I don't know make up a lot of sensational rubbish. My father is well-known, and yellow-press reporters have tried to sell copies in the past by suggesting we're jealous of each other. We both avoid publicity as much as we can, but I thought this might be a good chance to let someone write something impartial for a change.'

'And you think I'll be objective and fair?'

'I've seen most of what you've turned in, and I trust you to be objective.'

Sharon didn't know whether to be annoyed that he'd checked her work, or pleased that he thought her work was acceptable. She stared out of the window at the houses opposite. 'If your father won't mind, I'd be delighted.'

'Pick you up in half-an-hour? Where do you live?'

She gave him the address.

'Right!' There was a click and he rang off.

She re-dressed; dark-blue pants, a lapis lazuli sweater, and low-heeled shoes. It was cold so she grabbed a three-quarter length denim jacket and her outsize leather bag; she went to wait outside. It wasn't long before his silver BMW came into sight. Sharon was glad; the end of her nose was getting cold.

When she got in, he looked across and said, 'Why didn't you wait inside, I would have rung the bell.'

She shrugged. The car was warm and sheer bliss; it had comfortable leather seats, and a dashboard that reminded her of a plane's illuminated cockpit. Sharon felt slightly exhilarated to be with him on the way to his parent. She took a quick look round the opulent interior and said. 'Umm! Like it!' She met his eyes and noted his answer of flickering amusement. She coloured, looked down and fumbled around in her bag.

He revved the engine; it sounded a bit like a bear on the rampage. He effortlessly joined the flow of the traffic, and Sharon relaxed.

He looked sideways for a brief moment. 'I use this in bad weather, but I have an old MG — I'm an old-timer fan. There's nothing more exciting than driving down a country road with the hood off, and the wind tearing your hair out by the roots.'

She grinned, and was delighted that he seemed so relaxed. Trying to keep her voice pitched over the sound of the engine, which wasn't too difficult because the limousine purred along, she said. 'Lucky you, if you have a choice! I have a fairly dilapidated ten-year old Ford. I call it Louis XVI, because it is on its last legs! As long as I can get from my departure point to my destination without any trouble, I don't really care about appearance. I usually buy my Dad's rejects — then he can help me if it starts to play up! Men have a thing about cars, don't they? It's a bit like women and shoes. Sometimes human reactions are very illogical, aren't they?'

He sounded quite amused when he replied. 'Are you shoe orientated?'

She considered. 'Guilty! I have problems passing a window with gorgeous shoes, but generally, I'm quite happy with a simple life. Perhaps it has something to do with witnessing such a lot of unfairness in the world. It must be nice to own your own home, and have money stashed away in the bank, but money doesn't automatically generate happiness. Health, love and friendship is more important.' She hesitated, and hoped it didn't sound too hackneyed.

He stared solidly ahead, and said. 'You're right, but I think a lot of rich people are initially motivated by envy of others and by ingrained personal ambition. They don't seem to notice that ever-increasing stints of work bring financial rewards, but they have no time to enjoy it. They propel themselves away from the very thing they aimed for when they started out.'

Sharon fixed her sight on his fine hands on the steering wheel. He was a careful and competent driver. 'You're rich aren't you? Have your priorities changed? Perhaps they change automatically with growing affluence?'

They reached the outer edges of the business world and flashes of evergreen trees and the brown skeletons of leafless trees lined the roadways. She didn't think it was wrong to ask him about such things and he didn't seem to mind answering.

His dark hair glistened in the winter sunshine flooding through the window on his side of the car. Looking at him, she detected humour in the turned-up lips. 'Rich? How do you define rich — someone with half a million, a million, ten million, or a hundred million? I'm well-off but in comparison to most of my customers, I'm not. No one who buys my jewellery needs to worry about paying next month's electricity bill. That's one of the reasons why I wanted to produce fashion jewellery for T&M, so that people with lower incomes have a chance to buy something beautiful and well-designed too. If there were no rich people, I wouldn't have been able to take it on, or paste jewellery for opera performances.' Tongue in cheek he added. 'I still enjoy quite ordinary things like fish and chips, or a glass of beer in a pub, so I'm not completely degenerated yet.'

Not seeing the fun in his face, she continued. 'Oh, I'm not criticising. Everyone needs money; I just wonder exactly how much anyone needs to be really happy.'

'I'll watch my step, promise!' He paused and changed the conversation around. 'I notice you don't wear much jewellery. Is that your mute disapproval of too much affluence?'

Sharon laughed. 'Trust you to notice! I have a lovely pearl necklace that belonged to my grandmother, and a very good watch I got from my parents for my eighteenth birthday. I wear the watch constantly and the necklace when I go to formal occasions like weddings. I couldn't afford your kind of jewellery but I don't mind. I don't live the kind of life where I need it.' She paused, 'Someone like Blair is a perfect model for your jewellery isn't she? I like her, she's a nice person. Fame hasn't spoiled her.'

'Yes, I agree.'

They'd reached an area of large, detached houses. They stood regally, way off the road, and were surrounded by well-established gardens. Sharon viewed them with interest and stared curiously into the grounds, as they sped past. Patrick reduced speed and turned into the driveway of one of them. The wheels spun on the loose gravel as he drew up in front of the doorway. Dried leaves were tumbling around, and the wind seemed very cold after the warmth of the car. The dark green ivy, climbing up the stone façade, was quivering in the blustery weather. He got out and came around. Sharon was already out and waiting.

'Follow me!' He proceeded up the steps to unlock the door. He strode determinedly down the long hallway. 'Hello! Mum? Where are you?'

Sharon followed in his shadow and heard movements from upstairs. A wide, carpeted staircase swept upwards to the overlooking upstairs landing.

'Patrick! Here already? I'll be with you in a minute.' She looked down at Sharon. 'Hello, Miss?'

Sharon helped her. 'Robinson — Sharon Robinson — Sharon!'

The woman was a comfortable shape with a long salt-and-pepper thick plait dangling over one shoulder. Her nose was straight and short, she had an oval shaped face and her eyes twinkled down at them. 'Go out to the studio. I'll be down in a minute and make us some tea. I've got your aunt Agatha on the telephone, if I don't listen to her troubles now she'll phone back later on

47

— you know how your father hates being interrupted when he gets in front of the television!'

Sharon was amused. Her notion of a Bohemian way of life went by the board. His mother was just as mixed up in family politics as her own mother.

Patrick lifted his hand without commenting and carried on. The hallway was a connecting corridor; it trailed through the house to a doorway leading out onto a large flagged terrace. Crossing it, he went down a couple of shallow steps, across the lawn, through the windblown garden and on to a large conservatory. Sharon hurried to keep up with him. A man was moving around inside. Patrick turned the old-fashioned knob on the door and went in. The man looked up and a pleased expression flitted across his face.

'Patrick! Good to see you lad. How are things?'

Sharon's heartbeat increased when she saw how Patrick's good looks were augmented by a brilliant smile that displayed white uneven teeth. How nonsensical!

'Fine! And you?'

'Having a hell of a time with this figure, it's developing a life of its own. When I step back to take stock, I see something different every time.'

Patrick considered the half-finished form. 'It's good! I like it.'

'Really? If you say so, then I'm making progress. It's for a headquarters building up in Birmingham. A company wanted something for the entrance area. I was lucky to get the commission. I submitted a rough sketch, and that clinched it. Trouble is, now I find when I'm doing the actual carving, it takes me in a completely new direction all the time.'

Patrick laughed. 'That's nothing new is it? What's it called?'

His father scratched the back of his head. 'Outcry, or Protest — something like that! I can't remember exactly any more.'

'Why don't you send them a picture

from time to time, then they won't notice that you've freed yourself of the original design. If they don't complain when they see the various stages as you go along, they can't complain later about it not being the original design.'

'Hey! That's not a bad idea — sort of edge them gradually around to the new concept without them really noticing? I hate haggling with people when I've finished something and they try to tell me they expected something completely different.' He looked around and noticed Sharon, standing near the door. He did a double take. 'Good Lord!'

All of a sudden, Patrick's voice was tense for a few seconds. It was clear why. 'I know. I had that impression too — but it's just an initial impression. When you know her, that reaction disappears completely.'

Sharon's breathing quickened and her cheeks became warm. He'd adopted Andrew's wording. Her embarrassment changed to slight annoyance when the two men continued to stare at her as if she was a specimen in a test tube. His father broke the spell.

'Who exactly is this young lady, Patrick?'

'This is Sharon, Sharon Robinson. She's working on the PR project for the T&M contract I told you about.'

His father nodded absentmindedly. He was tall with greying hair and blue eyes. There were similarities between father and son, although Sharon couldn't define exactly what immediately. At the moment, he was wearing misshapen clothes covered in grey and white dust. He brushed his hands on the back of his things and came towards Sharon.

'Oh, yes — my wife told me just now that Patrick was bringing someone along. You gave my nerves a shake up for a few seconds young lady, but that was just a silly reaction. I'm pleased to meet you.'

She held out her hand. 'Hello Mr Caine.'

He clapped his hands together and a small cloud of dust was discharged.

Shaking her hand, he said. 'Can I show you round my studio?'

'No, no thank you. I'll just wander around on my own if you don't mind?'

Mr Caine waved his hands. 'Help yourself.'

'Mum's making tea.'

'Oh no!' He grumbled. 'I'm not breaking off now for a cup of tea.'

Patrick laughed. 'Carry on then. She's used to your unsocial behaviour, and Sharon won't mind, will you Sharon? She's getting used to putting up with grumpy people.'

She wandered, and looked at half-finished stone figures standing between piles of tools and rough blocks of various stones. Mr. Caine worked in the centre, where it looked a bit tidier, even if dust covered everything. Clearly, sculptors took more care of their lungs these days when they were polishing a figure — Sharon noticed a couple of face masks abandoned on the side. The two men continued to chat, standing near the unfinished figure, so Sharon slipped outside and walked round the garden, her hands stuck deep in her pockets. The wind played with her hair and sent bundles of multi-coloured leaves helter-skelter about her feet. Patrick's mother came onto the terrace and beckoned Sharon inside. Sharon shivered and was glad to join her.

His mother studied her carefully too, but perhaps women adjusted quicker, or she was too polite to comment. Sharon was fed up of the constant comparison and wanted to cut it out of the conversation. As she sat down, she said, 'People all say I look like Patrick's ex-wife.'

His mother looked at her honestly. 'You do, a little — but you're shorter, your eyes are a different shade and your facial structure is slightly different — you have a stronger chin and a straighter nose. I automatically analyse people's physiognomy. Their appearance often tells me a lot about the person's character.' She handed Sharon a cup.

'It sounds like you might be a bit of an artist in your own right?'

'I am. Not as well-known as the other two, but I have my own niche.'

'Oh!' Sharon was a little confused. 'I'm sorry, I didn't realise! Patrick didn't tell me. I'm not very well-informed about art. Until I got this job I've never had any direct contact.'

She smiled at the younger woman. 'If you've never been interested or had to get involved, that's not surprising. I'm a ceramic artist. Figures, groups, various themes, and individual forms as well. What do you do?'

Sharon explained and his mother asked a few pertinent questions.

'If you'd like to see what I do, I'll show you after.'

'I'd like that, very much.' Sharon smiled. 'No wonder Patrick is so talented! If both his parents are creative artists, he was predestined to follow in your footsteps, wasn't he?'

Mrs Caine shrugged and her loose clothes settled comfortably again. 'It was hard-going for Patrick. We never tried to influence him as to what he should do; in fact, I think we would have been almost relieved if he'd chosen to do something normal like working in a bank. Being the son of a ceramic artist and a sculptor definitely wasn't trouble-free. It took years until my husband established his name, and I wasn't prepared to give up my own ambitions either. Money was always scarce in the early years, and artists are terribly bound up in themselves and their work; they tend to drift away from reality sometimes. It took me a while to adjust to coping with my work and a small child. Patrick was independent from an early age, in a way other children weren't, because we were involved in our work. I'm sure his friends thought we were a little mad!'

Sharon nodded. 'But that's not a bad thing for a growing child, is it? Children who are spoiled have a harder time to fit in.'

Mrs Caine had a far-away expression

in her eyes. 'Perhaps — but looking back now, I think we should have made a greater effort to attend Patrick's sport's days, parents' meetings, that sort of thing. We should have found time to show a lot more interest in what he was doing generally.'

Sharon smiled softly and tilted her head to the side. 'I don't think he turned out badly, did he? He's successful, he's not introverted in the sense of not having any friends or interests outside his work, and he seems quite happy and satisfied with his lifestyle.' She paused. 'Losing his wife in that accident must have been a big shock — but he's coped with that too, and that shows strength of character. Even if you have occasional regrets, I don't get the impression that Patrick feels a bit of resentment. You all get on well; there's no trace of tension between any of you. In fact, I think he may have chosen an artistic career because he saw how you were happy doing what you do best. He needed to be talented, but he is, and he's doing extremely well.'

The older woman leaned back and viewed her young visitor thoughtfully. 'You think so? Well, I certainly hope so. Sometimes strangers see things clearer than you do yourself!'

The two men were walking leisurely towards the terrace.

Patrick's mother looked at them as they crossed the rough stone flagging. When they joined the two women, she said. 'Good heavens, Patrick. You managed to drag him away from his work for a cup of tea?'

His father looked at his wife indulgently, and then at Sharon to explain. 'I'm a bit of an irritable so and so sometimes, and not very polite either, I hope I didn't frighten you away with my remarks about Jessica?'

Sharon laughed softly and shook her head. 'No, of course not.' She tried to ignore the imposing figure standing silently at his side. 'I'm beginning to live with the fact that people are startled, or irritated, because I resemble

Patrick's wife. I don't like it much, but apart from dyeing my hair another colour and having plastic surgery, I don't know what I can do to lessen the effect.' She shrugged. 'It was a sheer coincidence that I got this job. Most likely the people who arranged it didn't have a clue about the similarity; otherwise they might have shown a bit more tact.' Her throat was dry, and she felt tense; she did every time Patrick's ex-wife was under review. It didn't seem to be getting better.

His father examined her more carefully. 'There are physical similarities, but they're not as strong as I first thought, and you're definitely a different character. My daughter-in-law would never have sat there having tea with my wife; she never had time!' His wife gave him a warning look.

Sharon wanted to ask what Jessica had been like, but couldn't. She gave Leon Caine a nervous smile instead. She saw no reason not to be honest. 'It's not enjoyable to be compared all the time;

especially when she was beautiful and I'm just average!'

Patrick looked at her pensively. 'Don't underrate yourself! Professional make-up and designer clothes can smooth out many rough edges.'

Did Sharon hear a note of irony in his voice?

His mother said, 'Now that you're here Patrick, stay for a meal. We don't see you enough these days. I've bought some steak and if you make some salad, we'll have a feast.'

He relaxed and smiled at her. 'Okay! You've twisted my arm.'

His father picked up his cup and saucer and turned to head back across the lawn. Speaking over his shoulder, he said, 'Call me when it's ready!'

Sharon got up and shouldered her bag. 'How do I get to the nearest bus stop? Or what's the quickest alternative way to get back into town?'

Mrs Caine answered quickly. 'With Patrick! You stay, I insist — there's plenty for all of us. You can't go yet; you haven't seen my studio.'

Sharon coloured slightly. 'It's very kind of you, but I don't want to butt in on a family meal.'

Mrs Caine brushed the words aside. 'We'll be delighted — we don't meet enough new people these days, and tend to hibernate with our work most of the time. If we didn't have to visit relatives, or talk to people who buy our things, we'd end up in a world of our own.'

Patrick hugged her briefly. 'Not as long as I'm around! Go and show off your bits and pieces to Sharon in your studio. I'll start in the kitchen.'

The longer she was with him, the more Sharon liked Patrick Caine. Outwardly, he was clever, intelligent, crisp, and dispassionate but his attitude softened completely when he was with someone he liked. He had sharpness and was unpredictable, but he wasn't half as callous as she'd initially believed. It was a pity that there was the barrier of his dead wife between them.

Mrs Caine touched her arm briefly. 'Come with me.'

Sharon followed, and they went up the broad staircase and another narrower flight of steps at the end of a corridor into a studio under the roof. Large windows had been put into the slanting eaves, and the room was flooded with light. There were low-level shelves along the walls and a large kiln dominated the far end of the room. A large heavy table stood in the centre, full of bowls, containers, brushes, tools and disregarded rubber gloves. Half-finished items were waiting for glazing or some other process. Standing regally, near the door, was a potter's wheel.

Sharon looked round with real interest.

'I make vases and other vessels, modern display plates, the occasional figure or group of figures. Lately I've started to produce whole dinner services on demand. They're based on environmental and architectural designs. I use carving and faceting technique to achieve interesting textures and appearances and I love strong-coloured beautiful glazes. I want my forms turned out to be elegant with fine crisp lines and deep colours.'

Sharon walked to one of the shelves with finished items. 'They're beautiful. They won't date. I love these plates with the delicate twig designs. Isn't it difficult to produce exactly the same size for a whole dinner service?'

His mother laughed softly. 'Ah! You need experience, a good eye, and a smidgen of luck. They are unique pieces, so no one expects exact measurements down to the last millimetre. They have to match, in appearance and size as far as humanly possible, and look good — that's the main requirement!'

'I like these vases too, beautiful colours. Blue is my favourite colour, and the various shades of blue in this one is just wonderful.'

'A good knowledge of glazing is the secret. Would you like to try the potter's wheel?' She bent down and switched it on; there was a faint buzzing sound in the air.

'Me? No thanks! You'll end up with clay on the ceiling or the floor. I'd rather watch.' She did; fascinated as she watched the older woman dip her hands in water and begin to shape some clay. 'It's obvious that if Patrick grew up in this kind of atmosphere that he found his own creative niche without even noticing it. He uses other materials, and other methods, but all of you are making something out of nothing, aren't you.'

Mrs Caine nodded and the wheel spun on.

Sharon could tell she was getting immersed in her work. 'I'll go and see if I can help Patrick.'

'Go ahead! I'll make a start on another plate. I have to have an order ready by the end of next week. Give me a call when you're ready.'

Mrs Caine was already completely absorbed by her task, so Sharon left quietly and went back downstairs.

4

After opening several wrong doors, she found Patrick at last. He was in a large, high-ceilinged kitchen with an old fashioned atmosphere. No slick built-in fixtures here. Half in anticipation, and worried in case he'd reject her offer, she said. 'I've come to help, if you'll let me.'

'If you like. What do you want to make?'

'The salad?'

He nodded. 'Over there — the lettuce is waiting to be washed; the cucumber and tomatoes are ready and waiting. You'll find salt etc. in the cupboard over there. I've just made a marinade for the steaks and I'm cooking the potatoes for fried potatoes.'

Sharon began to wash the lettuce in the white porcelain sink. A large wall-clock ticked away the passing seconds loudly. Out of the corner of her eye, she watched him as he went about his tasks efficiently. She said. 'You seem at home in the kitchen.'

His mouth curved into an unconscious smile. 'I like good food, so I either make it myself or go out. I prefer to cook most times and enjoy the end product straight away.'

'Your mother told me you were very independent from an early age, because both of them were so bound up in their work.'

An infectious smile covered his face and Sharon had to smile back. 'That's true, but I never felt it was a burden. I enjoyed the freedom of doing what I wanted to. Mum always cooked a meal when she had time, and the storeroom was always full of food. I probably ate too many sandwiches and fried eggs from time to time, but it made me appreciate good food all the more.' He looked out of the paned window, across the windswept garden. 'The weather looks good from in here but winter is looming with a vengeance, isn't it?' He turned and gave her a slow smile that gave her a tingling in the pit of her stomach. 'The potatoes are nearly ready; I'll get the big frying pan from the storeroom!'

Not long after they were all sitting around a wooden table in the dining room. Sharon was amused when Patrick called his parents a long time before things were actually ready. He explained it always took ages until they dragged themselves away from their work. When they arrived, his father moved in a cloud of dust as he slapped his trouser-legs on the way. His mother just patted her hair and adjusted her full skirt as she fell contentedly into one of the comfortable chairs.

'Open a bottle of that Chardonnay you brought us Christmas!'

'Good heavens! Do you still have some? Where is it? I can afford to have a glass too.'

It was an enjoyable meal. Sharon was content to sit and listen to family gossip about unknown relatives, and the inter-exchange of information about what they were all working on at the moment, and what was being planned for the immediate future.

Mr Caine leaned back. 'You're off to Hong Kong? How long this time?'

Patrick stretched and the muscles rippled under his soft blue shirt, and Sharon found that her thoughts were unmanageable for a moment. The news that he was going to Hong Kong was new, and illogically she didn't like the idea much. Why should it matter to her, where he went? She'd be out of his life forever, and working somewhere else in a couple of weeks.

Patrick shrugged. 'A couple of days; a week perhaps! The crew is scheduled to stay five days. I haven't decided yet. Perhaps I'll hang on a couple of extra days after the shooting is finished.' He noticed Sharon was puzzled and obliged by explaining. 'T&M are going to use Hong Kong as a background for the photos for the campaign.'

'That's a very exotic background.

They'll probably look wonderful!'

'I'll also visit some customers of mine in Hong Kong when I'm there, and I'll try to pick up some new commissions.'

She leaned forward and smiled. 'So you kill two birds with one stone?'

He smiled back and nodded; Sharon's heart skipped a beat again. 'The chain store pays my air-fare and expenses. I stay at my flat, and I can do business with my Chinese customers, between photo shooting sessions.'

'Do you have to be present all the time?'

He ran his long hand over his face. 'For the photo sessions? It's not absolutely necessary, but I have a say in how the jewellery is presented — it's part of my contract — so they know it's better for me to be around and approve, rather than to take photos that I'll throw out later. I can't complain later if I'm on the spot and have agreed!'

His mother joined in. 'When are you leaving?'

'Week after next, I think.'

She nodded. 'Don't forget to phone me when you get back home.'

He lifted his eyes to the sky. 'Mum, I am not a teenager anymore!'

She bustled, getting up to collect the remains of the meal. 'I know that, but there's nothing wrong with keeping in touch, is there?'

Sharon asked, 'Have you ever been to Hong Kong, Mrs Caine?'

'Yes, Patrick gave us a trip there for our fortieth anniversary this year.'

'And? Did you like it?'

She hesitated. 'It was terribly crowded, terribly busy, terribly hot, and terribly tiring — a different experience, but we did enjoy it didn't we, Leon?'

Patrick threw back his head and laughed. 'If I'd arranged for a week at a hotel in Bournemouth instead, you would have enjoyed it more. Don't pretend otherwise!' His eyes eyed her kindly.

It was late afternoon when they were ready to go. His father ambled off, and his mother came to the door to see them off. Patrick gave her a quick kiss on the cheek.

'Goodbye, Mrs Caine! Thank you so much for letting me come.'

She eyed the younger woman with interest, and picked up the vase Sharon had admired in the atelier from the nearby hall table. 'It was a pleasure. I hope we'll meet again. Here, something to remember me by!'

Colour flooded Sharon's face. 'Oh, I couldn't. It's extremely kind of you, but I wasn't trying to cadge.'

Mrs Caine tipped her head to the side and her eyes twinkled. 'I know that. I can tell if someone is or not. I enjoy giving something to someone who clearly likes it. I don't get much of a chance anymore; I'm dealing with anonymous companies these days.' She thrust the vase into Sharon's hands and smiled. 'Enjoy it!'

Still feeling a little confused, Patrick opened the door of the car and she got in, holding the gift tightly in the process. He revved the engine and sticking one hand out of the window to wave, he reversed back a short distance, until he could turn and speed off down the short drive. Sharon looked back at his mother, still standing in the doorway, and waved. His mother waved back and was then lost to sight.

She settled back into the seat and pitched her voice. 'I like your parents.'

'As a matter of fact, I do too! I've always secretly admired the way they enjoy their lives, even in the days before they earned much money from what they were doing.'

She nodded. She fingered the vase. 'It was very kind of your mum.'

He glanced sideways for a brief moment. 'She must have taken to you; she doesn't give things away right left and centre, you're honoured.'

There was heavy traffic on the way back, and Sharon was contented to just enjoy the journey. She looked out with pleasure at the autumn sunlight kissing the piles of multi-coloured leaves carpeting the ground.

His voice interrupted her thoughts. 'Have you ever been to Hong Kong?'

'No. America is the furthest I've got so far. I went there with my parents when I was twelve, and again with a friend when I was twenty.'

'Would you like to see Hong Kong?'

'Of course — who wouldn't? I'd love to see Hong Kong, Singapore, Australia; everywhere in fact.' She sighed. 'Perhaps I'll see some foreign places one day, if I'm lucky.'

Silence fell again and Sharon leaned back to enjoy the rest of the journey until Patrick drew up smoothly to the kerb.

'Thank you for inviting me today. I really enjoyed it.' She smiled and she was more than glad when he responded with a leisurely smile. Sharon had the feeling they were making progress and he was really beginning to accept her at last.

'I'm working this afternoon. What are you going to do?'

'I'll get some text down about contented families as long as it's still fresh in my mind, and Andrew has invited me to join him and a group of his friends this evening if I'd like to go.'

He nodded absentmindedly. He shook himself. It was none of his business what she did but he still felt a ludicrous twinge of annoyance at the idea of her being with Andrew's friends. He knew them all and often joined them himself. Sharon got out, still gripping his mother's vase.

Standing on the pavement, she waited until he drew out into the traffic again. In his rear mirror, he saw her still standing, until she turned and finally went indoors.

She liked Andrew's friends, they were all openly friendly and it turned out to be a good evening. To her surprise, Patrick joined them after a while. Clearly, he knew everyone and seemed at home with everyone. Andrew offered to take her home, but he'd come with a girl called Sandra, so Sharon decided to take her own taxi instead. Patrick offered to give her a lift too, but she refused — she didn't want to push her luck. She left earlier than most of the others.

★   ★   ★

Next morning there was nothing special on her agenda, so she began to polish her text on Patrick's visit to his parents. She never knew what would be used or not used later in the PR offensive, so she intended to treat every single theme as if that particular one was the most important one.

The phone broke in on her concentration. It was Andrew.

'Sharon? Sorry to bother you, but Patrick can't find a batch of designs he's finished for the T&M collection.'

Sharon was puzzled and waited until he went on.

'Patrick wondered if you'd seen them, or can suggest where they'd be?'

It took a few seconds for the penny to

drop. There were spots of red on her cheeks and she tried to stay calm. 'Why should I know where they are?'

Andrew hesitated. 'Patrick says the last time he can remember seeing them was the day you were in his studio.'

Sharon nearly exploded. Her tone was aroused and infuriated. 'Oh! I'm suspected of stealing his precious designs, am I?'

Andrew hastened to smooth things over and pacify her. He sounded slightly embarrassed. 'No, not at all! No one is accusing you, but it's pretty important for him to find them, and as soon as possible. I'm following up all the possibilities. If you were there when he last saw them, perhaps you recall seeing them?'

'Why didn't he phone me and ask me about his damned designs himself? Did he just pass the unpleasant work onto you?'

There was a short silence that spoke bands. 'He didn't honestly — and I don't think Patrick has even begun to think about the consequences if they don't turn up.'

'I haven't seen a single design of his on paper. The only paper I've ever noticed was a single sheet on his work-table that day I visited him in his workshop. I don't even know what was on it; it was too far away for me to see. Presumably it was the design of what he was working on at the time.'

Andrew's voice was a mixture of agitation and appeasement. 'You can imagine that the designs are all exclusive ones. If they got into the wrong hands, it wouldn't just mean Patrick would have to re-design the whole series for T&M, it also means someone out there would call his designs their own. There are plenty of people who'd love to claim Patrick Caine's work as their own, believe me!'

She was still bristling but she tried to stay calm for Andrew's sake. 'Sorry, I can't help I'm afraid.'

'It was worth a try! I was hoping you might remember something that would set us on the right path.'

'Sorry, I can't because I don't even know what they looked like!'

'Perhaps they'll turn up, or Patrick will remember where he had them last. I'll be in touch!'

'Yes — oh and thank you for inviting me last night, I enjoyed it.'

'Yes, they're a nice crowd. I'll let you know next time we get together; you seemed to fit in very nicely. Bye Sharon!'

'Bye, then.'

Sharon stared out of the window at the houses opposite. She chewed on the end of a pencil and thought about Andrew's call. Grabbing a short jeans jacket, a multi-coloured long woollen scarf that she wound round her neck a couple of times, and her shoulder-bag, she locked the door and headed for the bus stop — not even bothering to give her hair an extra brush.

Sharon rang the door bell and waited impatiently. She heard his footsteps coming across the box shape hallway.

When he opened the entrance door, he looked more than slightly startled to see her slender body, slim hips and irritated expression.

'Sharon! This is a surprise. What can I do for you?' A flash of humour crossed his face as he viewed the scarf enveloping her throat and most of her lower face.

Just dying to unload her annoyance, she ploughed into him. 'How dare you think that I am in some way responsible for the loss of your designs!' Even if he hadn't noted the pitch of her voice, her eyes told him how riled she was. 'And why didn't you phone me yourself about it, instead of asking your minions to do it for you?'

Taken aback, he opened the door wide and gestured her in. 'Before one of my neighbours call the police about a disturbance, you'd better come in.'

She marched past him, waited till he closed the door, and then with heightened colour she looked up at him again. She'd never have admitted it, but she was very happy to be indoors. Her nose, feet and hands were frozen. Rushing out, without giving any thought to the weather, was not a sensible idea at this time of year.

They were standing in the warmth of the hallway, with its under-floor heating. Patrick lifted his hand. The corner of his mouth turned up as he appraised her, and found himself forced to defend himself. 'I didn't ask anyone to do anything of the sort. Would you mind explaining? Come into the kitchen, you look half-frozen. I'll make you a chocolate drink.'

Sharon unwound the scarf, and tied it onto her bag. The prospect of a chocolate drink was very tempting, but it wouldn't put her off following up her intention. 'When I'm told that I was the last person who was around when you remember seeing the designs, and that they are now missing, that seems very much like finger-pointing to me!'

He ran his hand over his face to veil his expression. Her face was a picture of outrage. He stuck his hand into the pocket of his chinos and his lips quivered with hidden laughter. Determinedly he struggled to be serious. 'I'm sure no accusation was intended. I admit that I'm a bit haphazard about paying attention to the security side of my work. The last time I remember seeing them, they were bundled together with an elastic band and lying on top of the desk in the workshop, that morning you were here.' He turned and went towards the kitchen. Sharon followed. He busied himself with heating milk. 'I only tried to recollect where I had them when Andrew called, and he must have panicked, and asked you.' He added as a morsel of further information. 'Andrew tends to go to pieces about rights, and I think he can't sleep at night if he imagines someone else has their hands on my ideas.'

Sharon threw back her head and straightened her shoulders. 'Well, I don't like it! What would I do with your designs?'

He grinned and handed her a mug of

hot chocolate with a layer of whipped cream from a pressurised can. She cradled the mug gratefully and life was returning to her feet. She took a sip and it was nectar.

His mouth twitched. 'No, of course, I know so. Come down off your high horse Sharon! No one is accusing you; I didn't even know that Andrew was going to ask you. I'm not so yellow-bellied that I couldn't handle something like that myself, if I thought it was necessary.'

Her lips pouted slightly, she wasn't completely appeased. 'And — have you found them?'

'No, but I haven't really looked properly yet. I shouldn't be so offhand with them I know. I'll have to get into the habit of keeping them locked away if I'm not using them. I have a room with a security lock, and another large safe inside that again — where I keep the finished jewellery and the valuable metals, stones etc. I suppose I should stash the designs in there too, if I'm not using them.'

Eyes still over-bright, but her colour gradually returning to normal, she nodded. 'It sounds like you need an on-the-spot private secretary!'

'Do I?' His glance held hers. 'Looking for a job?'

'I'm getting plenty of money for doing very little at the moment already. You couldn't offer me more. Would you help me to search — now that I'm here anyway?'

He smiled. 'That's very magnanimous of you, considering you thought I was ready to deliver you up to the police a minute ago!' He enjoyed her slight confusion. 'Let's have breakfast; I haven't had any yet, have you?'

'What about the designs?'

He shrugged. 'They can wait. Never work on an empty stomach!'

The kitchen was compact with black and white tiles, and cupboards with high gloss finishes. Somehow, the room was typical of the man — cool elegance, clean uncluttered lines, modern and with smooth materials of modern technology. There was a breakfast bar built into the central cooking area and he began efficiently to rummage through the cupboards.

'Can I help?'

He looked up. 'Depends on what you'd like to eat.'

'I don't want anything; I've had breakfast already.'

'But you'll share a cup of coffee?'

He busied himself with a bowl of cereal and stuck a couple of pieces of bread in the toaster. In a matter of minutes, the coffee was bubbling in the machine and he was munching away comfortably. 'Sure that you're not hungry? I hope you're not one of these calorie counters?'

'No. I enjoy food very much.' She looked around. 'I like your kitchen it's very practical and stylish. Money does have its compensations, doesn't it?'

His mouth curved into an unconscious smile and he stood up to refill his cup. 'I work hard Sharon — it hasn't just fallen into my lap.'

She grinned mischievously, glad that they were back on normal terms again. 'I know that — I was just hoping to madden you more than a little.'

He stared at her and then burst out laughing. 'You are a strange woman. You came here breathing fire and brimstone and now you're trying to provoke me.'

Sharon tilted her head to the side, and realised that she liked Patrick Caine; she genuinely liked him. There were no rough edges to him, once you'd broken through his defences. The knowledge intrigued her and she wondered what he thought about her. The silence engulfed them for a moment as they eyed one another. It was interrupted by the telephone. He put his cup down and went out to answer it.

Sharon sipped her coffee and looked out of the window at the slightly neglected garden. One of the windows was open a little and she heard some birdsong nearby. She looked up as he came back; she noticed that he looked ill at ease. Glancing briefly at the ceiling, he looked at her directly and said, 'That was my mother.'

Sharon waited and wondered. He went on. 'She's found a bundle of my designs!' Tongue in cheek, he managed to look unconcerned. 'I must have had them in the pocket of my jacket when we were there, and they fell out.'

She stared at him in silence, and then burst into laughter. He joined her.

Sharon got up. 'Well, now that the mystery is solved, I'll leave you to finish your breakfast in peace.'

Rather sheepishly, he halted her departure. 'I think I owe you an apology.'

She shook her head. 'No, of course you don't. I'm just very glad that they've been found.'

Sticking both hands into his pockets and as casually as he could manage, he said. 'Come out with me for lunch!'

Her eyes widened. She was too startled by his suggestion to offer an immediate objection. She opened her mouth and then shut it again.

'I know a nice little place down by the river; it's quiet at this time of year. I'll just change into something more suitable, and then we can be off. If you don't mind, I'd like to pick up the designs from home first; we need them for some meeting or other in a day or so.'

She swallowed. 'And what about my appearance? In jeans an old T-shirt and a washed-out jacket! I don't think I've even brushed my hair properly this morning yet.'

He gave her a cursory examination. 'You look fine to me. You can borrow my bathroom for a while if it makes you feel better.'

5

The sky was an unfriendly grey. A spell of fine weather had finished and frost glittered here and there. Trees were withstanding the winter chill in stoic expectation of better things to come in a couple of months' time.

His mother smiled at them both as she opened the door; she motioned them inside.

The two of them automatically obeyed.

'We aren't staying, Mum — not for long anyway. We're going out for lunch. I have to pick up those designs. I've a meeting the day after tomorrow and they have to check the final details, before they begin production.'

Mrs Caine closed the door behind them. 'I thought you never wanted to get involved in mass production?'

Patrick led the way down the corridor

with Sharon at his heels. 'Oh, it isn't mass production. The jewellery is still a limited collection, but the materials are not lavish, and they are not handmade. In other words, they'll be expensive, but not completely out of the reach of ordinary earners if they want to buy something special. They'll be in the shops just before Christmas, and the campaign will continue into next year. It's an experiment, for me too. I'll find out if I can adapt my skills to produce beautiful, exclusive and less expensive items for the general public. My top customers will still get their classy, high-priced, and exclusive items. If I'm good enough, they'll still buy from me.' Patrick flopped down into one of the comfortable sofas. He waited for his mother's comment, and it wasn't long in coming.

'I just hope that your reputation for craftsmanship and quality doesn't suffer.' Her eyes were shadowed with worry, and one hand was deep in the pocket of her navy trousers.

'It won't.' His voice was as confident

as his expression. 'Jewellery is a bit like fashion. The haute couture designers in Paris produce fantastic single items in a limited number, but they have prêt-à-porter collections too, and they're a hell of a lot cheaper. Those collections make it possible for them to continue to work on exclusive items. They wouldn't be able to exist if they only sold their wares to the rich and beautiful; they don't sell enough, they're too exclusive.'

Mrs Caine nodded. 'I see what you mean.'

'If I can produce good quality designs in jewellery for normal customers in the same kind of way, I'll be able to go on producing the kind of exclusive items I love making, but which only a few people can afford to buy.'

Sharon added her comment. 'Did your involvement in making the jewellery for opera give you the idea?'

He eyed her speculatively. 'It probably did. I had to be sure that there was a market for it first. I'm fairly confident it will work without it chipping away at my reputation. The market research looks promising.' His arm slid across the back of the sofa. 'Where's Dad; in the studio?'

'Of course.'

'I'll just pop out and say hello. Where are the designs? We'll be off after; I haven't even booked a table, so we could be unlucky.'

His mother pointed to a sheaf of papers on a nearby Victorian sideboard. 'There they are. What will you do if they're booked out?'

'We'll come back here, and have baked beans on toast.' He nodded at Sharon. 'Want to say hello to my father?'

Sharon shook her head. 'No. I'll just wait for you here.'

He got up in a fluid movement and went out.

Mrs Caine used the chance to ask what she longed to know. 'Sharon, forgive my curiosity, but is something going on between you two?'

Sharon coloured bright pink. 'Good

heavens, no! Whatever makes you think that?'

'Patrick never talks much about his relationships with women, never did, but as he's brought you here twice within a very short time, I wondered if there was more to it than met the eye.' She paused.

Sharon's breath quickened and her cheeks became warm again. 'Patrick felt he had to invite me out to lunch after a misunderstanding we had about losing the designs.' Sharon explained what had happened.

Mrs Caine laughed softly. 'Oh, I see! Not that I would mind at all if you and he were a pair — it's none of my business. I'd like to see Patrick with someone who'd share his life and be good for him, and to be honest, you're the sort of person I was thinking of.'

Sharon shook her head steadily. 'Just a business connection — but I expect he'll meet someone again one day. He meets new people all the time. I don't think that he'll spend the rest of his life on his own.' Sharon looked down. 'At the moment the newspapers are linking his name to Blair Darleen. I've met her. She is a very nice person.'

Mrs Caine shrugged. 'We haven't met her, but I've seen the stories too.'

They were interrupted by the sight of Patrick coming back across the lawn, and they waited wordlessly until he came in to the room.

'When I mentioned I didn't want to keep you waiting, Dad could remember who you were, Sharon — and that's unusual.'

She avoided his mother's eyes.

He picked up the designs, and headed for the door again. 'Ready?' Addressing his mother, he said, 'I'll phone in a couple of days, okay?'

She nodded and, following them back down the hall, she continued to watch them speculatively as they got into Patrick's BMW and then drove off.

★   ★   ★

They reached the restaurant called Marco Polo, near Putney Wharf. Even though the scenery outside was proclaiming the approach of winter, Sharon had a feeling she was almost in the Mediterranean in the summertime when they went inside. The decor was soft pink and the lighting in the darker corners was orange. There were pleasant riverside views and the menu was in Italian. The restaurant was ultra glamorous and yet relaxed. The friendly staff waited patiently until they'd chosen their menu: an Italian salad, grilled halibut steak with butter and capers, and Tiramisu for desert.

An hour later, Sharon wiped the corner of her mouth and leaned back with a sigh. 'Oh, that was wonderful!'

He smiled and viewed the obvious pleasure in her face. 'Yes, I like this place too. Not just because of the cooking. The atmosphere is good.'

She stretched her back and leaned over the back of the chair. 'Thanks, Patrick! I don't think I'll eat again for a week!'

A soft light in his grey eyes showed

his amusement. 'I don't believe that! Tomorrow you'll be starving again by midday.'

She tilted her head. 'Do you know something; I think it's almost worth having a row with you; if I get invited out to lunch in a very select restaurant.'

He laughed and was surprised by how much he'd enjoyed being with her this morning. She was uncomplicated, interesting and had a great sense of humour, she also didn't have any allures — and that was something most of the people he knew thought was indispensable.

Spontaneously he said, 'Tell you what — I'll see if I can persuade them you should come with us when we go to Hong Kong.'

Sharon sat bolt upright and viewed him with an amazed expression. 'What! Do you think they'd agree?' Her eyes were wide open, brightly sparkling, and the colour on her cheeks heightened.

He shrugged and said casually, 'If I put some pressure on the people who have the final say it might succeed. I'll tell them it will be worthwhile to have descriptions of the shooting and background from someone on the spot. The woman in charge of the campaign thinks she has to pander to my whims — she has a soft spot for me. If they're prepared to send a whole team of photographers, models, make-up artists and advisers, one additional person shouldn't make much difference.'

The excitement grew as her mind thought about the possibility.

He eyed the sunny cheerfulness and buoyant expression on her features, and for some reason he felt slightly elated. Now that he'd got used to having her around, he had to admit she was a thoroughly nice, straightforward person. A trip to Hong Kong was almost routine for him these days. It would be interesting to see her reactions. Even if the company didn't agree, he'd make it possible. He looked out the window and suddenly wondered why he was prepared to go so far, for a relatively strange woman.

* ★ ★

The flight to Hong Kong was the longest Sharon had ever undertaken. Considering everything, the time passed quickly. She wasn't seated next to Patrick; her neighbour was one of the make-up team. She still felt excitement bubbling somewhere deep inside. She couldn't sleep but she did cat-nap now and then.

On arrival, the differences in temperature hit her when the group gathered outside the airport building to board the company taxi taking them from the airport into Hong Kong. The small bus had air-conditioning so she felt fresh enough to watch the passing scenery. It was difficult for Sharon to guess where Lantau ended and Kowloon began; skyscrapers were everywhere as the bus snaked along the coastline.

She was fascinated by the huge container port, the activity on the water, and the sheer mass of buildings everywhere. It was a fairly long drive, but everything was so foreign and new that Sharon's nose was glued to the window. Once they were in Kowloon the traffic was nose-to-tail, the buildings were nonstop, the advertising colours brilliant, and there were people rushing about everywhere. It was like being in a mountainous anthill, where everyone seemed to know where they were going and what they were doing. They were at their hotel before she realised it.

Getting out of the bus, the temperatures and high moisture content hit her like a blanket again. They gathered in the foyer, in an impressive reception area of huge proportions. Gold, marble, lots of mirrors, fountains, and dazzling lighting made Sharon blink twice. A local travel agent had been engaged to handle the details of their journey.

Waiting patiently, she sat down and studied her surroundings. Patrick was still with them; he was talking to the chief photographer but he smiled at her when he caught her eye. Sharon knew he wasn't staying in the hotel. He'd be in his own flat.

One by one, people from their party got their keys and disappeared. Her companion from the air-flight was sharing a room with someone else and smiled at Sharon as she went towards one of the lifts. The agent looked puzzled when Sharon still waited expectantly. He looked at her passport, in his hand. There was an animated discussion at the reception desk. Patrick was on his way out, but glanced at her and went to intervene. There was no reservation for Sharon Robinson. Even though Patrick pressured the staff, it didn't help. He came across and shrugged his shoulders.

'It seems there's a mix-up; perhaps it happened because your coming was decided at the last minute. There's some kind of huge international congress taking place locally and they haven't a room to spare. That's a pretty unusual situation; hotels always manage to push visitors in somewhere, even if they have no booking.' He ran his hand down his face. 'I expect you're feeling pretty tired by now?'

Sharon looked at her watch; it was almost 11 o'clock, and she'd left her flat at six the previous day to be sure to be at the airport on time. She nodded wordlessly.

'It'll take the agent time to find a room near here. The congress has filled up all the neighbouring hotels. If they put you in further away, you'll be isolated and won't be able to keep up with developments.' He paused. 'You'd better come with me. I have a guest room. You can get some sleep; and perhaps they'll sort things out for you later.'

Sharon's mouth opened and she shut it hastily. 'But — but I can't!'

He looked a little amused. 'Why not? Are you scared of me?'

She met his eyes. 'No, no of course not, but I'll be intruding on your privacy. I'm sure you don't want a stranger roaming your flat. There must be an alternative.'

'Probably is, but finding it might take

some time, and until then you'll probably fall over from sheer exhaustion. I wouldn't suggest it, unless I thought it would work! Where's your case? Follow me!' He strode off without waiting for her reaction, and Sharon made haste to follow. All the suitcases belonging to their party were piled on a nearby trolley, waiting to be delivered. Sharon hurried to point out which one was hers; Patrick already had his. The concierge organised a taxi and a bellboy loaded their luggage.

Once they were inside the taxi, Patrick said 'Braemar Hill — Temple Road!' The driver began to weave his vehicle through the busy traffic and eventually went through the Harbour Tunnel connecting Kowloon with Hong Kong Island. Once there double-decker busses, trams, cars and other taxis were all buzzing around them and Sharon could only gaze in excitement.

She turned to look at Patrick, sitting relaxed next to her. 'It is amazing! Another world, isn't it?'

He laughed softly, enjoying her enthusiasm. 'You're absolutely right — it is! I'm sure you'll like your stay. The majority of people are always fascinated the first time here, but after that, they either love Hong Kong or hate it. Some people can't stand the hustle and bustle. Basically, I prefer peace and quiet too, but I still love Hong Kong. It may seem sheer pandemonium to our European eyes, but everything is well organised. If it wasn't, anarchy would soon prevail. The place never ceases to inspire me. I've never gone away without some new idea bubbling at the back of my brain.'

Looking at the skyscrapers to the left and right as they passed the financial area, Sharon was reminded a little about driving through parts of New York in a taxi. This was completely different though; the streets hadn't been built in a grid-like pattern. Mostly they seemed to follow a higgledy-piggledy pattern, even though some were long ones. Braemar Hill was a steep climb; she saw no one on foot as they neared their goal. When they got out, Sharon looked up at a building that seemed to be touching the clouds. 'Good heavens! You live here?'

He grinned. 'On the seventeenth floor! But you have a view of the harbour from my living-room. The view was better a couple of years ago, until they built those other high-rise buildings in front of us.' He paid the driver and picked up their suitcases. 'This way!'

The temperature outside was warm and humid, and there was a foreign fragrance in the air she couldn't quite define. It was sweet; a mixture of exotic foliage, the water from the harbour below, and spices wrapped in balmy temperatures. It was foreign, but not unpleasant. Sharon didn't like to ask what happened if a fire broke out when you were on the 17th floor. Following him, she crossed the entrance hall towards one of the lifts. A uniformed guard recognised him as they went. He smiled at Patrick.

'Hello, Mr Caine! Long time, no see!'

'Hello, Hai-Long! How are things with you?'

The man nodded. 'Fine; and you?' He looked with interest at Sharon.

Patrick lifted his hand, the doors of the lift closed with a soft whooshing sound. Patrick explained. 'Most blocks of the more expensive flats have a twenty-four hour guard on duty. I thought in the beginning it was just making a job for someone, but now I realise how useful it is to have someone who controls all the comings and goings.' Sharon watched the lighted buttons indicating their upward progress. A soft bell announced they'd reached their goal and the door glided softly open. There were two doors facing each other.

Patrick fumbled in his pocket for some keys and opened the one on the right. 'The owner of the other flat on this level is an American who lives here for three-quarters of the year; a nice guy.' The cool air was welcoming and

Sharon was curious to see his flat.

He guessed so, and declared. 'Take a look around — it won't take long!'

The largest room was a sitting room with floor to ceiling windows, and a French window leading out on to a small balcony. Near the door, was a comfortable armchair, the rest of the sparse furniture was in neutral creams and whites.

From the balcony, through the gaps and over the tops of other buildings, she could pick out the turquoise waters of the bay down below. Looking sideways, there was still a strip of greenery on one side and then another high rise building beyond that, and there was another identical high-rise building next to them on the other side. Sharon sighed.

No hotel could have pleased her more. She came in and shut the door. She wandered around and found a compact kitchen with honey coloured cupboards and marble working surfaces. Another door led to a bathroom with a walk-in shower. Everything was in pristine condition.

Patrick dumped their suitcases in the tiny hallway, and pointed towards one of the doors while hanging up the lightweight jacket he'd been wearing. 'That's your bedroom, mine is next door. I hope you don't snore! The walls are not soundproof!'

Sharon took a quick peek at her bedroom. 'Nice!'

'It's not very big, but space is a cherished possession and property prices are sky high in Hong Kong.'

She said in confusion. 'I hope I won't cramp your style!'

His eyes twinkled. 'You couldn't cramp my style, even if you tried.'

Sharon turned away and picked up her suitcase. In her bedroom, she discovered a large bed already made up, a built-in wardrobe, a bedside table, a pot plant, lots of books in disorganised piles, and little else. She left her luggage and rejoined him. 'It's great — everything anyone could need.'

He was at the built-in fridge, and

took out a bottle of water. He checked the sell-by date and, pouring some into two glasses, he handed her one. 'It's not a showy kind of flat, but it's still expensive. A flat like this is almost unattainable for a normal Chinese worker.'

'How long have you been coming here?'

'About eight years. I bought this flat about six years ago. I came here more often in those days for longer periods, and I got fed up staying in hotels. I saw the advert for a new block of flats and bought one on impulse. Its price has trebled since then. You'll soon notice that Hong Kong never sleeps. Property prices, buildings, plans — it's all on the move twenty-four hours a day. The biggest problem I may face is that town authorities and investors may decide to pull down this skyscraper, get building permission, and proceed to put up a block of taller flats on the same spot.'

He looked at her, and to her complete surprise, he reached forward to tuck some errant hair behind her ear. 'You look tired. Why don't you get some sleep?'

Disconcerted, she lowered her eyes for a moment. When she looked up again, she was able to meet his gaze without any bewilderment. 'I think I will. Aren't you tired?'

He nodded. 'A little; but I slept on the plane for a bit. Before I get my head down, I'll go down to the market, and get us some essentials. Here's the spare key.' He took it from a drawer in the hall table.

Sharon took it, but said, 'It's not necessary — just for one day, is it?'

He didn't comment. Checking his wallet for money, he moved towards the door. 'See you later!'

6

When Sharon woke, the day was coming to an end. She hastily pulled on her jeans and straightened her wrinkled T-shirt and went into the living-room. There was no sign of Patrick. She went out onto the balcony and stood watching as the lights began to gradually appear on buildings everywhere. She was actually here, and it was just as fascinating as she hoped it would be. A soft click heralded Patrick's arrival. He hooked his long hands around the balustrade and stood silently next to her. They stood companionably side by side, both just enjoying the moment.

She broke the silence. 'It's wonderful.'

'I thought that you'd like it.' He turned to watch her. 'I phoned Clive earlier on.' Sharon remembered Clive was the main photographer.

'They haven't planned anything special for this evening. They're going to have a meal together, and then everyone is free to do what they want to do. They'll start photo-shooting on Lantau Island tomorrow. Perhaps it would be good for you to come tomorrow but you don't need to come every day. You can play tourist.' His teeth gleamed white in the semi-darkness.

She was relieved that she didn't need to join the others this evening. Most of them knew each other, because they'd often worked together before. 'I think I'll just stand here until tomorrow morning!'

He laughed. 'Much too tiring! I wondered if you'd like to walk about a bit. We can get something to eat, and you can have your first real experience of Hong Kong.'

Tentatively she said, 'Patrick, you don't have to show me around. I don't want to keep you from seeing old friends or acquaintances.'

'I wouldn't offer unless I think I'd enjoy it too.'

Something leaped inside, or her heart skipped a beat; she wasn't sure which — it was a silly reaction. She was glad that the semi-darkness hid the wave of pleasure in her face.

Sleep had refreshed her, and the temperature didn't sap at her energy now; daylight was waning and buildings were lit up everywhere. It was pleasantly warm; nothing could disguise the fact that this was foreign soil. She loved the atmosphere. She showered and changed. They walked down the street and passed a temple where a brief glimpse inside showed her huge incense coils hanging from the ceilings. The small back-street markets were brightly lit and doing a good trade. They wandered down towards the harbour and ate in an unimposing Chinese restaurant, where Patrick chose and she ate, with undisguised pleasure. They didn't talk a great deal, she was busy watching and absorbing. She grew wide eyed as he told her about the mid-levels escalator, and then they ambled along the shoreline to look opposite at Kowloon, and watch the illuminated harbour boats travelling back and fore on the water.

Patrick pointed to the Star Ferry on its never-ending journey back and forth between the island and the mainland. 'That's a must for any tourist, and only costs a pittance. You must see Hong Kong Island from Kowloon one evening too — that's another great attraction that costs nothing!'

She smiled up at him and brushed some strands of hair from her face.

He went on smoothly. 'You don't need to be at every photo shooting. One or two days will give you a good idea of what goes on. Use the remaining time to explore Hong Kong! I'll mark things in your travel guide, if you like.'

She said tentatively, 'Are you sure that no one will begin to complain if I don't turn up?'

He almost gave himself away. 'Why should they, when I've p . . . when they already know you only need a rough idea of how a collection is photo-graphed. No one needs to watch every single shot for five days. I won't either. I'm going to visit some of my Chinese customers and keep things on the boil.'

She nodded; eager to agree to his suggestions, and excited at the prospect of exploring. She wondered if it might be boring for Patrick to stroll along the waterfront and point out points of interest when he'd been coming here for so long, but he didn't indicate that it was a tedious task. That night she slept like a log, and she hoped she didn't snore.

★   ★   ★

It had other advantages, to be staying with Patrick; she didn't need to keep herself informed about details of their work. They phoned Patrick to tell him. Next morning she tried to remind him that she needed to find accommoda-tion, but he brushed it aside and said now she was here and didn't snore, it wasn't worth bothering further.

She didn't argue, glad that he didn't seem to mind her company — she presumed if he had, he'd move heaven and earth to find her a hotel room, near the others. She tagged along with him as they jostled through the multitude of other people hurrying everywhere on their way to work; it really felt like being part of some gigantic ant-hill.

When they arrived at the location, some of the people were already setting up cameras and discussing the light and the best position. Some indoor photos were being taken another day. She'd ask Patrick when, so that she could go there too. One or two models had travelled with them, but another additional two had joined them this morning. One of them, a beautiful blond with amethyst eyes and endlessly long legs rushed up to Patrick on their arrival and gave him a solid kiss that would have landed on his lips, if he hadn't moved his head at the last second.

'Darling! I haven't seen you for ages.

How are things?'

Patrick smiled in recognition and with an edge of amusement in his voice, he replied. 'Hi Gaynor! I'm fine, and you?'

She nodded. 'Just hunky-dory!' She looked with interest at Sharon, standing next to him. Her eyes narrowed, but she dismissed Sharon as a serious rival. 'We must go out for a meal one evening!'

He shrugged. 'I don't think there'll be time. I'm pretty busy every day, and I have a visitor staying with me.'

Clearly disappointed, Gaynor didn't give up so easily. 'You can't be busy with customers twenty-four hours a day, and if you have a visitor, dump them for one evening — just for me!'

Tongue in cheek, he replied. 'Gaynor, you know my income depends on whether customers want to buy my jewellery, just as much as your income depends on you presenting your sexy body as often as you get the chance for photos! I certainly wouldn't be so impolite as to dump a visitor, you know that!'

Sharon had an urge to intervene and assure him she didn't mind if he 'dumped' her one evening to go out with Gaynor, but he gave her no chance. He put his arm casually round Gaynor's shoulder. Sharon noted Gaynor was skilfully forming a disarming pout with her perfectly formed scarlet lips as she gazed up into his face.

Raising a smile, he said, 'Next time, perhaps? That's if I'm not married.'

She fluttered her long eyelashes at him. 'What difference will that make, my darling?'

Patrick tilted his head and met Sharon's eyes across the top of Gaynor's head and looked as if he was genuinely weighing the question. 'I know you can't understand that it makes a difference — but it does, Gaynor! As long as I was married, I toed the line, and I don't think that I'd react any differently if I ever marry again'.

Gaynor threw her arms around his neck. 'That's a very annoying attitude, but the solution is never to get married again. You're not married now Patrick, so let's enjoy ourselves!'

Sharon didn't want to listen to any more and moved away to look at the scenery. Down far below, container ships and other sea-going vessels were heading out into the South China Sea. They looked like toys on the water.

She tried to bury the feeling of annoyance she'd felt as she was watching Patrick with the model. She knew it was a stupid and silly reaction. Patrick was an artist, and he lived in a bohemian world. He met beautiful women all the time. Why shouldn't he feel flattered, feel attracted, get involved? It wasn't her personal idea of what love and commitment should be, but she didn't belong to his world. She took a deep breath and turned around. Patrick was disentangling himself from Gaynor's hold. Sharon looked for a place where she could watch without getting in anyone's way.

It was interesting, and she admired the professional attitude of all the people involved. The make-up artist from the plane journey saw her and came across for a quick chat.

'The high moisture content is murder. Every time I have someone's face bland and ready for a shot, the temperatures do their darnedest to sabotage things.' She threw a glance in Patrick's direction. 'How are you getting on with Patrick? I must say it was nice of him to offer you a room.'

Sharon met her questioning eyes straight and steady. 'Yes, it was kind, wasn't it? We get on fine so far.'

The girl's eyebrows lifted. 'I don't know him very well myself, but some of the others have worked with him in the past, and tell me he's turned into a bit of a recluse since his wife died — you know about his wife?'

Sharon nodded. 'Yes. Apparently, I resemble her a bit, and that caused some tension between us at first. He seems to have accepted it though, and he's perfectly friendly and normal now. I'm very grateful that he's put me up — I would have probably ended up a bit isolated from everyone, if he hadn't.'

The girl continued to eye him. 'There's something special about Patrick, isn't there? He's different to most of the well-known, successful men I've known. He has flair.'

Sharon didn't answer, and was glad when someone called the other girl away. Instead, she concentrated on the atmosphere, the surroundings and the action that was going on. Her immediate impressions had to provide a fitting text. She was glad she could sit in the shade and that Patrick had warned her to carry some drinking water with her wherever she went.

She felt uncomfortable when Gaynor sidled up and took a neighbouring seat in the shade. Her clothes were the last word in elegance, her brows high and shapely, her facial bone structure perfect, and her figure couldn't be faulted. Sharon knew nothing about skin tones, but she guessed that Gaynor's would be perfect to display the various pieces of jewellery Patrick took out of the small leather case he'd brought with him. Gaynor leaned back and massaged the back of her neck with her scarlet tipped fingers.

In comparison, Sharon felt like someone who was visiting the city from the country; the two of them were the veritable city and country mouse. This morning her lightweight red and white skirt and simple white top had seemed fresh and smart, now she almost had a feeling she was wearing a cast-off from a second-hand shop.

She straightened her shoulders and shook her head; what did it matter what she looked like? No one here noticed. She didn't want to admit to herself that this morning she had taken extra care as she dressed, because she was going out with Patrick. 'You know Patrick?' Gaynor's voice was low and very pleasant.

Sharon looked at her. 'It depends how you define the word 'know'. I've been working with him for a couple of weeks, but it's not a personal relation-ship, if that's what you mean.'

Gaynor nodded. Sharon had a fleeting impression she was relieved. 'What do you do?'

Sharon explained.

'Hmm! Not a bad idea. Even if they only use bits of it, it will probably show Patrick in a more personal way, make things easier for the PR people. He's brilliant!'

Sharon looked down at her hands and was silent.

Gaynor continued. 'You look a bit like Jessica; do you know that?'

'Yes, everyone says so.'

Gaynor cadged a cigarette from a passing photographer and blowing a cloud of blue into the air above them, she said. 'Jessica was a butterfly. She lived life to the full. I think it got too much for Patrick sometimes. I've been friendly with Patrick for a couple of years, and I know it looks like I'm chasing Patrick like a loose hussy, but I really like him.

Sharon wondered why Gaynor was baring her soul to her — a complete and utter stranger.

120

'He's a gem.' She sounded sincere. 'Patrick's wife was someone who knew how to paint the town red. I know how to enjoy life myself too. Patrick is different; he is capable of having fun and enjoying himself, but I've never seen Patrick out of control. Still, I think any woman would be prepared to change, if it meant she could belong to Patrick in the end.'

Sharon felt uncomfortable. 'I've never even seen a good photo of his wife, so I can't comment.'

Gaynor considered her for a moment. 'If you straightened your eyebrows, cut a couple of inches off your hair and put some gold tints into it, lost two or three kilos, and wore the smartest clothes anyone could afford, you'd be very similar.'

Sharon was irritated. 'I'd never dream of trying! What for? It was a fluke that Patrick and I ever met. He's been very kind to me on this trip — I agree with you, he is nice.'

Someone called Gaynor for the next shot, and Sharon was glad. She decided to leave the set and go for a walk. There was no point in watching every single photo being taken. The pieces of jewellery were chosen to their best advantage. When the models changed, they did so in full view of everyone, discarding their outerwear and hopping around in unbelievably skimpy under-wear, before slipping into whatever dress they were given.

To Sharon it was a strange world. Sharon couldn't imagine what it would be like to stand practically naked in front of strangers all the time.

She didn't join the others next day; she made for some of the tourist points Patrick had suggested instead. Patrick was gone before she was up and ready for breakfast. She could afford to take her time; she watched the traffic on the harbour's turquoise waters through the gaps in the buildings, while cradling a mug of coffee in her hands.

Once she was on her way, she could see it was going to be a sunny, cloudless day — so she looked at his suggestion list and decided to go up to the Peak. On her way up in the tram and while she was enjoying the journey, she thought about the meal they'd shared when they got back to the flat last night. Neither of them had felt like going out and Sharon was glad when he had suggested that they make a meal and stay in. It was simple, just a steak with salad, but it couldn't have tasted finer if they'd been in the best restaurant in town. She'd felt perfectly relaxed with him, and they'd chatted about themselves, about their pasts.

Sharon noticed he'd avoided mentioning Jessica, but that was all right with her. They'd sat on the narrow balcony afterwards. There was barely room for two chairs and she could have easily brushed his bare arm resting on the arm of his, but she'd been careful not to. It had been the best part of the day — the temperature had gone down with the sun, and there had been a feeling that the organised, energetic, anthill was beginning to slumber. Most people were relaxing after a day of tiring work. They'd shared companionable silence between unrevealing conversation, and Sharon found that he was a thoroughly nice, intelligent man and she'd never felt quite so relaxed with anyone before.

When the tram reached the summit, she was rewarded by a breathtaking view of the Hong Kong skyline, and she joined all the other tourists trying to capture the moment with their cameras. She sat there for a while, relished her visit, enjoyed a cup of coffee nearby before taking the return journey to the base again.

* * *

When she got back to the flat late afternoon, her trousers felt clammy and she was glad to have a shower. Without having any intention of sleeping, she stretched out on her bed and was soon dead to the world. She didn't even stir when Patrick returned. After looking elsewhere, he opened her bedroom door to find her sprawled carelessly on top of the covers sleeping like a child, and his face creased to a sudden smile. He closed the door softly and went for a shower.

When Sharon emerged, he was sitting in the living-room surrounded by papers and some pieces of jewellery. He smiled automatically as she came in. 'I didn't hear you come back! How long have you been here?'

He stretched lazily and the shirt tightened across his chest. 'Long enough! You were sleeping, so I left you to it.' Sharon wasn't sure how she felt about the idea he had been watching her in her sleep, so she ignored it.

'Would you like some tea, or coffee?'

He nodded. 'Let's be very British, or very Chinese, and drink tea.' His dark grey eyes followed her for a second until she disappeared into the kitchen, then he turned back to his work again. He put it aside when she came back with a loaded tray.

Leaning forward with his forearms

resting on his thighs, he asked. 'Where have you been?'

She busied herself with the tea things and replied, 'The Peak, the Financial District, Hong Kong Park, Government House and all the other bits in between.'

Curious, he asked, 'Didn't you go shopping?'

'Just a quick look in some of the European style department stores — but it was mostly to cool down for a while. I did buy something though.'

'What was that?'

Sharon went to fetch it, and handed him a small oblong box covered in Chinese silk. She sat down and watched him open it. 'A name chop; I have one too — in wood. This one is jade, of course.'

She swallowed tightly as he dropped down beside her, and handed it back. Their fingers touched and she tingled from the contact. He'd never been so close, and a faint light twinkled in the depth of his dark eyes. Sharon told herself her reaction was perfectly natural — he was very good looking, and she was feeling slightly euphoric because although he'd had problems accepting her presence at first, he now seemed to have accepted her completely.

He stood up. 'A name chop is a very traditional object; they used them to sign official documents. Some companies and small firms, still use a name chop today. The Chinese uphold traditions and old beliefs. A lot of them believe in fate and divine intervention.'

She took a sip of tea and came back to earth. 'Yes, so I've read.'

'Do you — believe in fate, luck, destiny — or whatever you like to call it?'

The question intrigued her.

'I don't know. I wouldn't dismiss the idea totally, but everyone can make the best out of their lives. It depends a lot on your own character. Two people with exactly the same chances and choices end up with completely different results.

'I wouldn't put everything down to fate, although sometimes it would be nice to believe you had no choice in the matter. You wouldn't need to blame yourself then if things go wrong, or if you have bad luck. Do you believe in destiny?'

His voice was level and slow when he replied, 'I'm inclined to think there's more to it than most of us want to admit.'

He picked up his cup, and the mood lightened when he asked, 'Shall we go across to Kowloon this evening? There are some quite decent restaurants along the waterfront and you can take a look at the Hong Kong skyline by night.'

★ ★ ★

Once there, Sharon admitted the view was terrific, but she didn't try to take photos. Patrick had already warned her that unless she had an excellent camera the pictures would probably turn out blurred. She bought some postcards at a kiosk run by a friendly Chinese woman. They managed to get one of the tables facing the skyline, and after a brief wait, they were able to order.

Sharon sighed softly as she sat back and took it all in. 'This is something to remember always. The Star Ferry, the Skyline, the tourists . . . '

'And me?' He fingered her postcards and waited.

She smiled easily although her emotions whirled and skidded. 'And you, of course! Without you, I wouldn't be sitting here, would I?'

He looked down. 'Who are the postcards for?'

'My parents, my brother, Andrew, some girls I know, my former boss, Clive, one for your parents — if you give me their address — the kind of people who would send me one if they were on holiday. Look at this one showing ancient Chinese pottery; your mother will like that, I'm sure.'

'So everyone gets one but me?'

She accepted the banter. He was a complex man who was sure of his place in the universe but she was finding that he evoked conflicting emotions in her. 'Do you want one? What for? You know

Hong Kong better than I ever will. But I will send you one if you like; one with a Chinese dragon — a dragon brings luck, doesn't it?'

Sharon found his presence disturbed her in an ever increasing way. She had no intention of permitting herself to fall under his spell, in a couple of weeks they would part and she'd never see him again. That idea bothered her more than she cared to admit. She lifted her glass. 'Here's to us; here and now.'

He responded, and his slow smile only warned her further that she had to keep an iron control on her emotions. If circumstances had been different, she might have relaxed and enjoyed being with him without worrying about the future, but she was the last woman in the world to attract Patrick physically, not when she reminded him of someone he'd loved in the past. She concentrated on being cheerful and showing him how glad she was to be in Hong Kong, in his company.

Patrick was amused when she insisted

on paying for the meal, but he didn't make a fuss, and she was grateful that he probably understood that she wanted to contribute financially to her share of their entertainment.

Sharon went to the photo shooting next day, because it was taking place in one of the shopping arcades. Everyone appreciated the air-conditioned atmosphere and the work seemed to flow easier. Claire avoided talking to Gaynor, but she doubted if the model wanted to chat with her, even if she'd had the chance. Patrick wore a short-sleeved white shirt and stone-coloured jeans that fitted his lean frame perfectly. He looked satisfied with the progress they were making and had a commanding air of self-confidence. His beautiful, long-fingered hands chose the jewellery to match the clothes with a certainty born of knowledge and instinct. He never attempted to single her out in any way when they were part of the working group; she didn't expect anything else.

The photographer's assistant, Mike,

occupied some of the time between shots talking to her. He was amusing and charming and she felt a little flattered that he'd singled her out. With so many beautiful faces to choose from it gave her day a boost.

A couple of hours later, Sharon had had enough and when she caught Patrick's eye briefly, she signalled to him that she was going. He lifted his hand in acknowledgement.

She strolled through some of the shops on the way back, and bought a skirt that caught her eye. Passing a newspaper stand, she glanced at the headlines of the glossy magazines; she was torn by conflicting emotions when she read that Blair Darleen had announced her engagement to an Argentinean tenor. She wondered if Patrick knew. It was hot outside, and she enjoyed the Star Ferry trip back to Hong Kong Island.

Hemmed in by the gleaming sky-scrapers, she decided to go up to the Peak again. It would be cooler up there and she'd take an easy walk around the shoulder of the Peak. She was rewarded by seeing verdant valleys and the South China Sea and the outlying islands beyond.

Her thoughts skimmed the last couple of weeks and she began to wonder what she really hoped for and wanted of Patrick. He was generous, and gave her a lot of everything, but not of his real self. Would she have stood a chance to attract him if she hadn't resembled Jessica, and they'd met under other circumstances?

Impatiently she pulled her drifting thoughts together. Why should he have ever singled her out, even under other circumstances? She was a perfectly ordinary woman; he met models, artists, the rich and the beautiful all the time. Her thoughts reminded her that his name had been linked to Blair Darleen in recent times. Would he be upset by the news, or just move on to another girlfriend with a shrug of his shoulders?

Back at his flat, she was startled by

the phone ringing. Undecided whether to answer it or not, in the end, she did. 'Sharon Robinson, for Patrick Caine; can I help you?'

There was laughter in his voice. 'And this is Patrick Caine speaking, informing Sharon Robinson that I'm going out with the others for a meal.'

Flustered by the sound of his voice, she hurried to form a reply. 'Patrick! Oh! Thanks for letting me know; it wasn't necessary.' Sharon was glad of the chance to mention Blair without having to watch his face. 'Patrick, I saw a magazine today that said that Blair Darleen had announced her engagement to a tenor.'

There was a slight pause. 'Oh! It's out is it? I knew it was on the horizon months and months ago, but they've managed to keep it secret.'

She was relieved that he didn't seem to be put out. 'Really?'

Sounding unconcerned, he explained 'I've known Blair for a couple of years, and she asked me if she could use me as a cover-up now and then to keep the paparazzi off their tails.'

'Oh, I see! Enjoy yourself this evening!'

There was amusement in his voice. 'I will.'

There was a click and they were disconnected.

Sharon made herself a sandwich, watched TV, and went to bed early. She vowed not to listen for his return. Sleep evaded her, so she sat in bed reading a paperback; she put out the light and settled down, as soon as she'd heard movement in the hallway.

7

He'd left before she emerged next morning; she remembered him mentioning he intended to look up some of his Chinese customers today, so she presumed he'd be busy until late that day. Sharon mused that it was her last full day. Tomorrow lunchtime they'd be on their way home again. She'd use her last chance to visit something of special interest today. She went to Lantau to see the giant Buddha.

It was late afternoon when she got back to the flat, she had a shower and then started to pack her suitcase. She heard Patrick's key in the door and her heart skipped a beat. When he came in, she spotted his arm in a sling. He looked awkward and began to explain.

'I didn't look properly when I was crossing the road. A small truck came around the corner just as I was stepping off the kerb. It wasn't his fault. I slid across the bonnet and landed ignominiously on my rear end.' Sharon's eyes were wide. 'I've been to the hospital and had an X-ray. They think my shoulder may have a hair-line fracture; I have to go back tomorrow to see someone who has more experience in shoulder injuries.

Sharon felt a bit like a fish which had been landed, and was now gasping for breath. She pulled herself together. 'Sure you're all right? You can't afford to have an arm injury!'

'I'm sure it is nothing serious.' He threw a newspaper he'd been carrying on to the hall table and went into the sitting-room. On the way, he said, 'I'd love a cup of tea though!'

Sharon was glad to do something. 'I'll make it.'

'The doctor recommended the sling for a day or two — for extra support.'

Sharon busied herself in the kitchen. When she came back with the tray, she said, 'We're due to leave tomorrow. Will you be able to travel?'

'As I've begun treatment here, I'm going to hang on for a day or two to clear things up. At home, I'd only have to start from scratch again.'

She nodded, poured him a cup of strong tea, and shoved the sugar and milk in his direction. She hoped it wouldn't sound too egoistical when she said, 'The train to the airport leaves from near the Star Ferry pier, doesn't it? Will you be able to manage on your own?'

There was a slight hesitation; his eyes were hooded when he asked, 'I'll manage, but I'm hoping you'll hang on for a day or two with me. One good arm is enough to manage, but having someone else who'll substitute for me if necessary would be a godsend.'

She looked up quickly; her mind was spinning. She didn't hesitate; there was nothing she'd rather do. 'Of course I'll stay. Are you sure you wouldn't prefer someone else?'

'Who?'

Her mouth was dry. 'Oh, I don't

know, but some of the others have known you much longer, and I'm sure they'd help straight away if you ask them.'

'Perhaps, but I'm asking you.' Patiently he waited for an answer.

'Right, that's settled then.' She took a sip of tea, smiled shakily, and put the cup back onto the saucer with a rattle.

He looked amused. 'You're more jumpy than I am.'

'Is there anything we have to do? What about the air-tickets? Perhaps they can be re-booked? It's an awful lot of money to lose for no reason.'

'They are clear-cut bookings, nothing to do with special rates or anything like that, so it shouldn't be too difficult to transfer. If not — ' He shrugged. 'Once we've finished tea, I'll try to sort it out, and then we'll go out to eat.'

When they were leaving the building, a Chinese man in clean working clothes came up to them and thrust a package at Sharon. He accompanied the gesture with a cascade of Chinese. She held back, waiting for someone, to explain what it was all about.

Patrick studied him. 'I think he's the truck driver from this morning but I can't be sure. It might have something to do with that.' Patrick went inside to fetch the guard, and they all listened to the man again. The guard explained the man wanted to show his gratitude. If Patrick hadn't accepted responsibility, it could have had had serious consequences. It would have been disastrous; he had a family and elderly parents to support. Patrick tried to brush his thanks aside, but the man was determined. He gave them a toothy smile and with an added sentence, he nodded his head, thrust the package at Sharon, who took it, and then he turned and walked away.

'What did he say before he left?'

The guard said, 'He wished you constant happiness and many children!'

Sharon coloured and looked down at the small parcel, packed in plain brown paper and tied with string.

Without further comment, Patrick

said, 'Well, go ahead! Open it!'

She did. It was a jade amulet. Obviously old; it had probably been in his family for generations. Patrick examined it briefly.

'Hmm! It must have been hard for him to give it away. I don't suppose he has a lot of anything to spare.'

'Then let me run after him, give it back.' Sharon could still see the man walking along off down the street.

Patrick shook his head. 'You can't do that, he'd feel insulted. He wanted to show his gratitude; you can't rob him of that now.'

'It's very attractive. But it's yours, not mine.' She held it out to him.

'He thought we were a pair, and he thought you belonged to me. He gave it to you, not to me. Let's not test the will of the gods. Perhaps it really will bring you luck and happiness.'

With her mouth half-open and not knowing what to say, he tucked his healthy arm through hers and pulled her gently to his side.

* ★ ★

Next morning she felt elated that she wasn't on her way to catch the plane, and that she could be with him for a day or two longer. Luckily, the damage was the left shoulder, so he had no trouble shaving or getting himself ready.

'Does it hurt?' She poured him coffee, and indicated towards his toast which he was clumsily trying to spread with butter and marmalade.

He nodded. She took the slice of toast and completed the task.

He picked it up and munched contentedly. 'A bit; but it's not so bad this morning'.

'Then it'll sort itself out soon, I'm sure. Can I come with you to the hospital?'

He gave her a friendly, bantering smile and seemed completely relaxed. 'If you like, but you'll be bored. You'd be better off here.

When he emerged from the treatment rooms, she experienced the constriction of her throat and a quickening of her heart beat that happened every time she saw him coming towards her now. It was something new — she'd never felt like this about anyone else she'd ever met, and Sharon knew it meant she was falling in love with Patrick, and there was nothing she could do to stop it happening. She could only hope to hide it from him.

He looked smug. 'They can't find any noticeable damage, so it's just bruising after all. I should wear the sling for a day or so, but by the time we fly, it should be unnecessary.'

She looked at her wristwatch. Their original flight had left, and Patrick had booked them on a new flight on the coming Monday. That left them with the weekend.

'What would you like to do?'

'Me? What you would recommend.'

'Let's go to one of the outlying islands this afternoon? Cheung Chau is my favourite. The ferries go there from the central pier, on Hong Kong Island.

It's not a long journey, and we can walk around the island easily and perhaps have a meal before we come back?'

It was a lovely afternoon. The ferry crossing alone was worth the trip. There wasn't a cloud in the sky. Cheung Chau had managed to keep some of its original Chinese charm. No traffic and it still had a fishing fleet. Their walk looping the whole island was exceedingly enjoyable. He checked his long stride to match hers and she had loads of time to take lots of photos. Patrick told her about some of the various outlying islands, and it was clear that his fascination with Hong Kong hadn't lessened with the years.

Sharon had a problem with seeing the fish she'd eat swimming in a tank beforehand, so she ate noodles and vegetables but Patrick had no qualms, and also managed his knife and fork quite well. The waterside restaurants on the island were simple, with simple tables covered in plastic tablecloths. There weren't many non-Chinese around, and that made the experience even more exotic.

When they got back to the flat, it was twilight and the illuminated buildings decorated the skyline. They sat on the balcony with a drink and Sharon had a tingling in her stomach — it happened all the time whenever she was alone with him. She didn't want the day to end. She was so close to him, she could feel the heat of his body. Sharon found it hard to believe when he described how Hong Kong would soon be decorated with Father Christmas, and Christmas trees, and all the madness of the Christmas season. It was a hangover from colonial times, and the people of Hong Kong continued to celebrate it to the full. She was sitting next to the door. When her glass was finally empty, she got up.

'Goodnight, Patrick! Thanks for a lovely afternoon.' On impulse, she leaned across and kissed his cheek. She couldn't guess what he thought. She only hoped that by giving in to her own longings she hadn't overstepped the mark.

He didn't make a movement, but

after a moment of silence, he simply said, 'Goodnight!'

She went indoors and left him alone with his thoughts and also the night.

★ ★ ★

Facing each other across the breakfast table, Sharon found it impossible to gauge Patrick's expression. She was astonished at the sense of fulfilment she felt being with him, but how did he feel? He could smile with unexpected good humour, and then his handsome face looked detached again. His self-command, studied relaxation, and politeness, made it difficult for her to guess what was really behind the mask.

Patrick coped without the sling while having breakfast. It took him a little longer, but things seemed to be improving already. Sharon had made them some scrambled eggs and he finished his portion with obvious enjoyment.

'Anything you'd like to do in particular?' She shook her head.

'Let's go shopping then!'

She tilted her head and smiled. 'I don't know many men who would suggest that to a woman.'

His dark brows arched mischievously. 'It's helpful to know what's happening in the fashion world. If I produce jewellery that doesn't match, I'd be wasting my time. Main colours change from season to season, etc. etc.' An easy smile played at the corner of his mouth.

Her feelings for him were intensifying, and they had nothing to do with reason. However much she told herself to be careful, his nearness overwhelmed her, and she was unable to wrench herself away from her ridiculous pre-occupations about him.

After clearing the breakfast things, they gathered their things and set off. They went down with the escalator, and sauntered through the various exclusive shops in buildings in the Financial District. Once inside, the air-conditioning made things enjoyable.

Sharon found most of the exclusive

fashion on show not to her taste; it was too extravagant. Standing in front of one display dummy dressed in a bright red, short skirted, sophisticated creation, she commented. 'I can't imagine ever wearing something like that!'

His voice lacked emotion when he said, 'Jessica bought extreme fashion all the time. Eventually she had a huge wardrobe of unusual clothes; she loved to stand out in a crowd.'

It was the first time he'd spontaneously mentioned Jessica. She hesitated, and her heart thumped quickly, before she stared up at him and said. 'It's a good thing that we're all different.'

'And to think I was considering buying it for you!' he joked.

She gave a soft chuckle. 'Liar!'

After wandering the shops for a while, they took the Star Ferry to Kowloon, and walked the short distance to the Peninsula Hotel. He told her, 'Everyone should take the chance to have afternoon tea in the Peninsula; it's a must.'

Once they were settled, she looked

around. 'If I ever come into money, I'll come back and stay here!'

He nodded and laughed. 'Not the cheapest place in town!'

When they came out into the bright sunlight, he was ahead of her. She stumbled and he reached out with his free arm to steady her. His gaze was rivetted on her face and he searched her eyes. She felt a lurch of excitement when he lowered his head and kissed her, leaving her mouth burning with fire. His other arm was in the sling between them, but even with just one arm, Patrick managed competently to hold her close.

Raising his mouth from her, he studied her reaction. Her desire for him overrode everything else and must have been mirrored in her face. His second kiss was feather-like and held a tantalising persuasion that made her wish it would last forever. He was still holding her, but he then let his arm fall away, and stepped back. He seemed momentarily taken aback.

Sharon's breath quickened and her

cheeks grew warm.

Someone tried to get around them to pass, and broke the spell. He moved ahead and she followed. She longed to reach up and touch where his lips had been, but didn't. They reached a gap on the busy pavement and he chose his words carefully when he turned to face her. 'Opportunity makes a thief! I didn't mean to hassle you.'

Her breath caught in her throat and she wished she'd had enough courage to say she wished he'd hassle her more often. Instead, she gave him a shaky laugh. 'No hassle; no harm done!'

He gave her a quick disturbed smile, glad that she was helping to gloss things over. Sharon didn't believe for a second, that he'd planned, or intended to kiss her; it had just happened.

*   *   *

There was still a little tension in the air but they both wanted to avoid wondering why, or to discuss it. By the time they got back to the flat, it was late afternoon. Sharon escaped to her room, with a few bland words about having a cat-nap; she was more shaken than she cared to admit. At least she now knew he found her attractive enough to want to kiss her.

A short time later, the doorbell broke the silence. Sharon heard a familiar sounding female voice. Should she stay, or join Patrick? In the end, she joined them. She wasn't really surprised to find Gaynor draped elegantly across a sofa. Gaynor took in Sharon's slightly 'just got up' appearance, and patted her own perfectly styled blond hair.

'You know Gaynor?' The arm sling hung vacantly on his chest.

She looked at Gaynor. 'Yes, we've met.'

He nodded. 'Gaynor and my wife were friends; she lives in Hong Kong. Like something to drink?'

Gaynor was playing with a tumbler of orange juice, and Sharon felt Gaynor was also watching her carefully through hooded eyes.

Sharon answered. 'Water please!' Accepting the glass, she sat down and resigned herself to being a polite listener. Patrick remained standing.

Addressing him, Gaynor said, 'I heard that you were forced to prolong your stay: I was passing and thought I'd find out how you were.' She drained her glass and the ice tinkled as it fell back into the tumbler.

'Oh — I'm fine! They thought it was a hair-line fracture, but it wasn't. We're leaving the day after tomorrow.'

Gaynor nodded and held out her glass. Patrick said, 'Sorry, no more orange juice. Water?'

Gaynor pulled a face. Sharon was glad of an excuse to leave them for a while. 'I'll get some from the corner market; won't take a minute.'

Patrick opened his mouth to protest; Gaynor didn't. Sharon hurried out and grabbed her shoulder-bag on the way.

★   ★   ★

She walked back from the market slowly, opened the door and heard Patrick laughing. She put her bag back on the hall table and walked towards the living-room. The door was open a crack and she heard Gaynor saying. 'She's clearly besotted with you Patrick, and I expect you'll enjoy taking advantage of the situation and bringing it all to a successful and romantic conclusion before you leave. It's to be expected I suppose, both of you cooped up in the flat together like this.'

The colour drained from Sharon's face, and a glazed look began to spread. Her fists clenched and her nails dug into her palms.

Patrick's voice drifted towards her. 'She's unique; I haven't met anyone so refreshingly unsophisticated for years. It's very invigorating.'

Gaynor gave a throaty chuckle. 'I bet, and I also bet it won't take you long to convince her that the rest of her time here can't be used in any better way than to be head-over-heels in love with you, in a comfortable bed with a bottle of champagne.'

Sharon didn't want to hear any more. She fled to her room and sank down on the edge of the bed. A chill surrounded her. Had that been Patrick's intention from the beginning? Gaynor had known him for years. Had he been kind and considerate so that she'd be lulled into wanting to pay him back with her body? She didn't want to believe it, but he hadn't contradicted Gaynor. She eyed her half-packed suitcase and sprang into action. It didn't take her long to add the rest of her things and lock it. Parking the suitcase outside the door, she left her plane ticket, the bottle of orange juice and the spare key on the hall table. Hoisting her shoulder bag and simmering with anger, she opened the living-room door. They looked at her guiltily, Patrick more than Gaynor. Sudden stains of scarlet covered Sharon's cheeks, and then all colour drained away. Even though her throat was dry and blocked by a lump, that seemed the size of an orange, when the words tumbled out, rancour sharpened her voice.

'Thank you for your hospitality Patrick. I heard you talking about me so don't pretend that I wasn't the topic of the conversation.' Silently he held up his hand to protest.

She ploughed on, her eyes glistening, and couldn't hold back her spite. 'I may seem naive in your eyes, but I'm not a fool, and I think too much of myself to make myself cheaply available for anyone, especially someone who couldn't care less about me as a person. I won't be around for bedtime adventures with you today or any other time. I'm sure Gaynor will be willing to oblige. I won't tax your hospitality any longer. Have a good journey; I'll find my own way home.'

They stared at one another across a sudden ringing silence and he looked shocked. He made a move towards her, but Gaynor got up and blocked his way, reaching out to grab his sleeve and hold him back.

Sharon turned on her heel, and

hurried as fast as her legs could carry her through the hall and out of the door. Their loud voices followed her to the lift. She swallowed hard and bit back the tears. Her first task was to find a travel agency so that she could fly home as soon as possible. She might have to book into a hotel until there was a vacancy.

She didn't take the normal route they used to walk down to the waterside; she went in the opposite direction, in case he tried to follow when he noticed she'd packed and gone. She found an empty taxi, cruising and looking for a customer. With relief, she let the driver load her suitcase and got in. She told him she was looking for a travel agency in Kowloon, and he murmured something about a friend who worked in one, on Nathan Road. That was fine. She wanted to get off Hong Kong Island as soon as she possibly could.

The travel agency was full of Hong-Kong Chinese; and they were all talking at the same time. Sharon was used to the high volume of shrill chatter by now, and was glad. Silence would have been harder — given her time to think. When it was her turn at last, she lugged her suitcase to the desk, and explained what she wanted, the young Chinese woman picked up the phone and dialled.

A couple of minutes later she said, 'There are still some seats on a plane leaving at 10pm for London.' She looked up at the wall clock. 'If you leave now, you have plenty of time to get to the airport. The next possibility is tomorrow morning, and that's not a direct flight.'

Desperate to be on the move, she took out her credit card. 'I'll take it'.

8

When she got back home, the weather matched her mood. It was grey, cold and hostile. The journey had been the longest and most miserable one she'd ever make. She was unable to sleep, and when she looked in the mirror next morning, there were dark rings under her eyes. They weren't just due to tiredness; she was exceedingly miserable.

She'd tossed and turned thinking about Patrick; weighed up her own blind love for him, against his casual attitude. She recalled how he didn't mind play-acting an affair with Blair Darleen for the press, and his devil-may care attitude to someone like Gaynor. It hurt to admit Patrick wasn't the kind of partner she needed. She needed a life-time partner. Patrick would drop her without a qualm when someone who attracted him more came along.

He'd disapproved of her in the beginning, but then she'd been silly enough to believe he'd felt attracted to her in Hong Kong, but it looked like he'd merely been setting her up.

She went straight to the T&M's buildings the first day back. She wanted to hand in her text about the photo sessions. She asked to be released from the contract as soon as possible. As the people in charge had plenty of text, the date for the presentation of the jewellery was looming fast and they had masses of other problems to solve, they agreed without a moment's hesitation. Sharon didn't remind them about their promise to help find her a job, she didn't want to stay in the city any more, she wanted to move far away from Patrick and never see him again.

Back in her small rented room, she packed her possessions again, sent the key back to the reception desk at T&M with a short explanation, and a few hours and a telephone call later, she was on her way home to her parents.

The streets were full of Christmas illuminations as the taxi sped past, en route to the station. Now and then, she glimpsed into the heart of someone's home. The warmth, the decorations, the sight of people smiling and children laughing, made Sharon wonder miserably if her own life would ever seem worthwhile again.

She felt drained and overwhelmed. One way to cope with misery was to find a new job, as soon as possible. She'd immerse herself in work; that might help. She was filled with bitterness and sadness but she was glad that her pride was intact, and she hadn't made a fool of herself.

Despite all endeavours to shut Patrick out of her thoughts and heart, it wasn't that easy. The hurt was like a sick and fiery illness gnawing inside. If her parents noticed something was very wrong, they were clever enough not to quiz her about what it was. Sharon was endlessly grateful for that. She couldn't talk to anyone about Patrick — not yet.

One evening she had to stop moping in front of the TV screen when her father told her Andrew Bryce was on the phone and wanted to talk to her.

The colour shot to her face, and she straightened her shoulders as she picked up the receiver — not knowing what to expect. 'Andrew? Hello! How do you know my parent's telephone number?'

The sound of his familiar voice brought a weak smile to her lips. 'The Human Resources department at T&M had your parent's address — you must have given them as next of kin when you filled out your application.'

There was a pregnant pause. 'Something went radically wrong between you and Patrick in Hong Kong didn't it? Since he got back, he's like a bear with a sore head; he's closed up like a clam, and buried himself in work. I wondered if I can do something to put things right? Does it have something to do with your resemblance to Jessica?'

She floundered for a moment but finally managed. 'No, I honestly think he got over that some time ago. As the newspapers would say, we have now discovered insurmountable differences.'

'What happened?'

'I'd rather not talk about Patrick if you don't mind. It's nothing dramatic. I've finished doing the job I was paid to do, and now our paths go in different directions again. I wish him all the best, and every success.' Sharon knew that it was true. She still loved him too much to ever want anything but the best for him. She swallowed hard and managed to ask. 'How are you?'

'Me? I'm fine. What are you doing these days?'

'I've just applied for a job in the editorial department of a small magazine. It doesn't pay much, even in comparison to the newspaper I used to work for, but I have to earn a living. I'm moving back to my own flat at the weekend, so you were lucky to still find me here.'

'I thought you always wanted to work in the city?'

She shrugged into the telephone, 'I did too, at first. Now I think I'm not really suited to city life.'

'But you'll come up to London now and then?'

'Perhaps, on a visit!'

'Then phone me when you do; we can have lunch together. I'd like to keep in touch.'

Sharon laughed quietly. 'Okay, I will.' She didn't really want to, because he'd tell her what Patrick was doing. But she didn't want to hurt Andrew's feelings — he'd always been good to her. 'Anyway, how's the campaign shaping up now?'

They talked a bit about the on-coming public presentation in two week's time. When she put the phone down, she felt drained.

★   ★   ★

A few days later, she moved back to her own flat. It didn't help because she was alone in the silent rooms after work.

She didn't yet feel like contacting old friends. The following weekend she visited her parents and stiffened when her mother handed her a letter with Patrick's writing that had arrived that morning. She stuffed it into her pocket and deliberated; she tore it into small pieces and threw it in the bin on her way out, without reading it. She told herself it was the sensible thing to do; it was better not to react, and forget him — she would, one day.

She got the job; it was on a monthly magazine on gardening, hobbies and the home. She worked her way into her tasks, and although it meant a longer drive, at least she didn't need to move from her present flat. She decided to offer to help out in a local youth centre; it would fill some of the evenings, and divert her thoughts. She had to get her life back on an even keel again.

She got an ornate invitation to the launching of the Patrick Caine Collection taking place on the shortest day of the year. At first glance, she rejected the idea, but there was also an appeal to come, in Andrew's handwriting reminding her she'd indirectly worked on the promotional text, and he wanted her to come, for his sake. She hesitated, but figured that if she arrived late and left early she wouldn't need to speak to Patrick. Her magazine was closing down for the Christmas holidays anyway, and starting up after the New Year. She needed an additional day off to attend, but when she explained, her new boss agreed.

She wore a favourite dress — a very simple white shift with three-quarter length sleeves, smart black high heels and a warm long camel-hair coat on top. Her dark hair shone; she fastened it in a black velvet bow. As ever, she used make-up sparingly. Winter had the country in its grip. Tree tops glistened and people's breath exhaled in grey clouds on the icy air. The occasional blizzard was causing transport delays, but her train journey was fast and trouble free.

On her way to the T&M head-
quarters, she noticed that Christmas bustle
was in full swing everywhere, and there
was a constant stream of Christmas pop
music pouring out of all the supermar-
kets and department stores everywhere.
Sharon hadn't thought much about
Christmas yet, and it was almost on top
of them. Perhaps she should try to do
some present buying before she caught
the train home.

She dawdled outside the headquarter
building; the cold was biting her nose
and she was getting cold feet — but she
still needed to kill a little more time.
Checking her watch at intervals, she
eventually entered the reception area
and produced her invitation. She was
directed to the top floor. Her breath
caught in her throat when she saw
Patrick's face on some of the posters
decorating the long corridor. The hum
of voices reached her long before she
arrived at the room. The press was
taking photographs, there was a sound
of glasses clinking, and cosy groups

were talking and laughing. The room was crowded and Sharon saw some familiar faces and lots of unfamiliar ones.

She threaded her way towards the department head who'd handled her texts. Sharon listened as she chatted about how the campaign had finally culminated in today's presentation. Someone called for silence and to Sharon's relief, the official part of the event began.

Sharon had longed for, and was also afraid of the moment when she actually saw Patrick again. She found he was now standing on a low podium with a group of other people, all of whom were strangers to her. He looked tough, lean and sinewy, and her breath caught in her throat. He was dressed in black like the first time she saw him and it emphasised his beautifully proportioned body and dark hair.

Until this moment, Sharon thought she'd made progress in accepting that he'd never be hers, but fresh anguish grabbed at her when she looked at him. Her face felt stiff and unnatural when he spotted her. A muscle clenched along his jaw as if he was annoyed, or angered, by the sight of her standing there. The lines of concentration on his face deepened, then his neighbour forced his attention elsewhere.

When the introduction speeches began, she looked among the crowd to find Andrew and threaded her way to his side. Tugging at his sleeve, she was rewarded by a smile. She whispered. 'Hello! I kept my promise, but I can't stay for long.'

'Oh, come on! I can't believe that! You must give us a chance to have a bit of a chat!'

Sharon looked up at the podium and noticed Patrick watching them. 'No, the weather was bad on the way up, and I don't want to get stuck in town overnight — I'm taking the first train home after I've done some of my Christmas shopping.'

The people around them were clearly

irritated by their whispering and gave them disapproving glances. Sharon shrugged her shoulders, and smiled at Andrew. 'I'll phone you after Christmas, promise!' She withdrew, moving steadily back towards the door, and storing the picture of Patrick smiling politely at someone on the podium who was introducing him as she crept out, closing the door as silently as she could.

She sighed with relief. She had come, kept her promise to Andrew, and done her duty by showing her face at the presentation. She began to make her way towards the lift at the end of the long corridor. It was decorated with publicity posters showing the jewellery, and there was one she would like to have taken with her — Patrick in his apartment. The walls were also decorated with Christmas decorations, and she was reminded of her intention to do her Christmas shopping.

She'd probably never see Patrick again; her throat ached with defeat at the thought, and she swallowed the despair. She walked on in lonely silence and all animation left her face as she thought about a future with no Patrick. The sound of her high heels in the empty corridor echoed as she went. On the way, the door to the ladies room opened, and Sharon came face to face with Gaynor. It was hard to say which of them was more surprised.

Sharon rallied first and said politely, 'Hello!'

Gaynor looked at her, lifted her perfected shaped blond eyebrows and managed to reply through stiff lips. 'I didn't expect to see you here today.'

'Didn't you? Andrew asked me to make a special effort so I did. It is only a flying visit; I have another appointment.'

'And Patrick? Have you seen Patrick?'

Sharon paled. 'I saw him just now, on the podium. I think he saw me but I don't suppose he expects me to wait for a chat. There are lots of other people who'll make demands on his time.'

Gaynor was silent and a circle of disapproval circled her mouth. She eyed

Sharon and put an end to the growing tension. 'Do you know something — you don't deserve him! I can't understand why he's hooked on you, but he is. Why don't you give him a chance?'

Feeling slightly stunned by her words, Sharon's heart lurched. What was she talking about? She set her chin in a stubborn line. 'You don't need to praise Patrick to the gods! You were both making fun about how 'besotted' I was with him before I left, and I'm quoting that!'

The colour in her face deepened and she ploughed on. 'You were also picturing the idea of how willingly I'd share his bed before we left Hong Kong. I didn't hear Patrick protesting or denying it. You were enjoying yourself at my expense. Why should I want to talk to Patrick, or you if it comes to that?'

Gaynor eyed her carefully. 'Patrick tried to find you, after you left like a scalded cat. He used all his contacts, and mine, and eventually found out you'd left the same day. I've never seen him so angry and I realise he'll never forgive me for what happened. Our friendship has cooled to minus zero.'

Sharon was infuriated by pent up emotion; she retorted angrily. 'There was no reason for him to go to so much trouble. He spoke the truth that day when he said I was naive. From his point of view, I am.

'But I'm not so naive that I can't take care of myself. I don't mind being labelled naive if that means believing in love and commitment. I don't like the sort of world where two-timing, cheating your partner, or sleeping around is probably considered a harmless pastime. We have different attitudes. No harm was done, and I have no doubt that he'll find enough girlfriends who suit him much better. I don't need to discuss anything with him; it wouldn't change a thing.'

Gaynor's voice was heavy with irony. 'If you weren't so completely tied up in your own anger, you'd recall that Patrick used the expression 'refreshingly unsophisticated', or something similar. He never said you were naive; there's a world of difference in the meaning. I noticed straight off that he was interested in you in a special way, and other people did too.

'I admit I tried to drive a wedge between you two by making fun — because I was madly jealous! When you eavesdropped, you should at least have eavesdropped to the end, and heard how angry Patrick got. He threw me out, and told me never to come back again. It must have been a struggle for him to phone me later to ask my help to find out where you'd gone — I know a lot of people who work at the airport. I think he was scared you might not have enough money to buy a ticket home, or to pay for a hotel. He was immensely relieved you were safe; when he finally found out you were on a plane home.'

She looked at Sharon and scowled;

the expression ruined her exquisite beauty. 'I've known him a long time, and I'd cut off my right hand to belong to him. You can't even be bothered to talk to him! You're being plain stupid Sharon; you're throwing away the best man you'll ever know!'

Not giving Sharon a chance to reply, Gaynor turned away and went back down the hallway towards the opening ceremony without a backward glance. Sharon had to admit that behind the flawless make-up, perfect figure and pampered skin, she was an ordinary woman who was passionate about someone she really loved — and that someone was Patrick Caine.

Sharon was glued to the spot for a few minutes. Thoughts tumbled around in her brain. She was tempted to go back to the presentation and confront him — but it was the wrong time, and the wrong place. She also needed to be sure about what she wanted; how far was she prepared to go? She left the building and walked down tree-lined streets with their Christmas lights swinging in the wind. Gaynor loved Patrick, because she wanted to make Patrick's world right, and Sharon was prepared to do that too. Had she acted too impulsively; assumed, and blamed him for something that wasn't true?

She joined the bustle in the department stores, partly to get warm, and also hoping to forget her dilemma. After wandering around for some time, and uninspiringly thinking about buying her mother a bottle of perfume for Christmas, she knew today was not the right day for her to do her shopping. She found a bistro down a side-street and sat mulling things over. After a couple of coffees, a final glance at her wristwatch told her she had to make a decision; either to catch the next train, or try to see Patrick and catch a late one.

She checked the train connections for that day on her list. Folding the paper and shoving it back into her bag, she made her way out. It took her several minutes to find a taxi. She reckoned that the presentation must have finished hours ago, and hoped Patrick wouldn't go somewhere else, before returning home. She felt she had to face him now; she'd never feel happy again if she didn't do that. She gave the taxi driver Patrick's address.

9

Leaning back into the leather uphol-
stery, Sharon hoped that fate would be
kind to her. She didn't expect him to
completely understand why she'd bolted,
but she had an urge to at least put
things right between them again; she
hated the idea that he thought badly of
her. Patrick was fair-minded; she knew
he'd give her a chance to explain. She
paid off the driver and stood in front of
the familiar house. It was already dark.
The sky was clear, stars were twinkling
high above and a frosty oval moon was
on the wane. If she wasn't mistaken,
there was snow in the air. She took a
deep breath and climbed the two shallow steps to the door. She rang the
doorbell, and heard it echoing inside.
Waiting, it seemed to take an eternity,
and Sharon's heart had already begun
to sink in despondency with the thought

he wasn't at home after all when suddenly she heard footsteps approaching, and her depression was replaced by a feeling of slight panic. What if he didn't want to see her again?

He opened the door and a wave of warmth from within enveloped her. They stood facing each other in silence. Patrick drew defensively into himself when he saw who it was; the skin drew tight over his cheekbones and his dark eyes seemed to burn in his face. He looked tired. It had already been a long, nerve-wracking day for him, and now she was standing on his doorstep and he probably couldn't imagine why.

She didn't know where to start and became increasingly uneasy under his scrutiny. 'Patrick — Patrick, I'm sorry. I overheard you and Gaynor that day and I got the wrong end of the stick! I really did think you only wanted to have your fun at my expense.'

He drew a long breath and came to life. He reached forward to take her arm and pull her inside. 'Come in!'

She did. Once inside, he let it fall again before he led the way into the living-room. Sharon followed. Cushions were rumpled on one of the sofas, and Sharon guessed he'd been lying down when she'd arrived. 'I've disturbed you?' She gestured towards the settee.

There was a faint glimpse of old humour when he said. 'You haven't stopped disturbing me, ever since we met! Take off your coat!'

He helped her and she did. He threw it over the back of a nearby chair. Blood pounded through her veins and her face grew hot. Their closeness was like a drug; barely a few seconds in his company and she was already beginning to feel the inner excitement and notice how the thudding of her heart was increasing by the second.

His eyes narrowed speculatively. He asked abruptly. 'Why didn't you answer my letter?'

She gave him the truth. 'I — I didn't open it. I ripped it up without looking at the contents and threw it away!'

She watched him as he ran his hands over his face and then snapped at her. 'You threw it away? Once I dug out your parent's address, I thought I could explain — put right what I guessed had gone wrong. I begged you to get in touch so that we could sort things out rationally. I also said if you didn't contact me, I would take it as a sign you wanted nothing more to do with me and wanted to be left alone!'

She paled at her own stupidity. She hadn't given him the slightest chance. Her stomach was clenched tight. 'I'm sorry . . . but I felt dreadfully hurt and offended by what I heard that afternoon. I wondered all the time if my similarity to Jessica was behind everything. Perhaps I was merely rousing pleasant memories in you, providing you with a way of having her back, and your friendship had nothing to do with me as a person.'

In a lightning movement, he reached forward and pulled her into his arms. 'Do you realise how miserable not having you around has made me for the last couple of weeks?' The ends of his words were smothered on her lips and his kiss sent the pit of her stomach into a wild swirl. 'What I feel for you has absolutely nothing to do with Jessica — I swear it!' His lips recaptured hers again, and were more demanding.

Sharon felt her knees weaken and her senses whirl. She felt wrapped in a covering of invisible warmth and her heart danced with excitement. Happiness began to fill the dark comers. She'd dreamed of being crushed in his embrace, and reality was better than fantasy.

His hands moved down the length of her body as if he were making sure she was here and real. His features grew more animated when he noticed the sparkle in her eyes. His whole face spread into a smile and her answering one was full of affection and delight. He reached out for her hand and pulled her down next to him on the nearest sofa. Wrapping his arm around her shoulders, he turned towards her.

'I think before we talk about anything else, we have to take some time to talk about Jessica.'

Sharon took a deep breath and steadied her smile. He was right; her ghost was between them.

'I can't pretend that Jessica never existed. She was a part of my life, and we were even happy together for a while. Can you accept that?'

Sharon nodded. 'Of course, I know that. You wouldn't have married her unless you loved her, would you?'

He resumed. 'We weren't happy for long. Our marriage was short and towards the end, I wondered what was holding the threadbare strands together. We wanted completely different things from life. I don't know what would have happened if she hadn't died; most likely we would have ended up getting a messy divorce.'

She swallowed hard and lifted her chin. 'It's probably wrong to be jealous of a dead woman, but I am! It's hard to accept you loved someone else.'

He pushed a strand of hair behind an

ear and kissed the tip of her nose. 'I've thought a lot about us; I haven't stopped thinking about us since we met. Why did I feel drawn to two women who were similar in looks? I think you and I were meant to meet, sometime, somewhere. Perhaps fate mixed the two of you up, and I met Jessica first, by mistake?'

Sharon tried to lighten the direction he was taking. 'You mean destiny got its links crossed? That's going a bit far isn't it?'

He shrugged. 'Who knows? I just want you to understand that Jessica is yesteryear. She isn't an icon, I don't have her on a pedestal, and I've come to realise my feelings of guilt about her death may have something to do with the fact that I felt a kind of relief that it was all over. Does that sound brutal? I certainly wasn't looking for a replacement, but as soon as we met, the wheels began to turn — even if I was disgruntled and antagonistic towards you in the beginning. You are you, and I want you.

'You have no reason to be jealous of Jessica. You've had boyfriends, you mentioned them now and then, and I don't like the idea of you with another man, but I know deep down that it doesn't really matter. We matter, here and now matters, nothing else does!'

Even though her feet seemed to be drifting along on a cloud, she managed to utter some sensible remarks. 'We're not terribly suited are we? That might cause problems in the long run. Your world is full of glamour and excitement, and mine is rather mundane in contrast.'

He stared at her and then burst out laughing. 'My world is just as mundane as yours and everyone else's. I have to sell what I make, and I'm involved with all sorts of people who help me achieve that aim. Sometimes I enjoy what's involved in publicising my work, sometimes I don't. The best part for me is always my work. With you at my side, I'll be even happier to close the door on the rest of the world and forget it whenever I can. I don't need the presentations, the parties, the invitations, but sometimes I have to get involved.

'Perhaps one day I may be so famous that my name will sell anything I make, anywhere in the world, without all the personal appearances. If you take me on, that's something you have to accept — but you come with me wherever I go, otherwise I won't go.' He paused and kissed her again. Looking into her happy face, he suddenly asked. 'What actually changed your mind and brought you here today? I was feeling as miserable as anyone can get. I saw you at the presentation and you slipped away.'

'I met Gaynor in the corridor, and she told me I was being a fool.'

He looked amused. 'Did she? Good for her! Gaynor pushed us apart, but she seems to have helped to iron things out in the end so I suppose I ought to be grateful to her for that. I can never forgive her for driving us apart in the first place though.' He grew serious. 'I love you Sharon, I never expected to, but I love you with my whole heart and soul. You can't imagine how unhappy I've been because I thought I'd lost you forever.'

She snuggled up and laid her head in the crick of his shoulder. 'I can, I was just as miserable. I dare you to lose me ever again. I think I've loved you for weeks and weeks; it's been growing gradually but I know that I'll love you for the rest of my life.'

'Good! Can you stay?'

She looked up. 'Here? Now? The last possible train leaves at 10.30. I was planning to be on it.'

'Not any more. Now that I've got you back again, you have to stay. I'll drive you home tomorrow morning — perhaps I can meet your parents? By the way, my Mum's got your card from Hong Kong in a prominent place on the mantelpiece and keeps drilling me about where you are, and when she's going to see you again.'

He shrugged when she remarked. 'It looks like snow out there!'

'Good! I hope it is three foot high tomorrow. Then you can help me decorate the tree, and make it the best Christmas ever. Is this new job of yours so important? Couldn't you find something near here; or better still take up freelance journalism instead?'

'Perhaps! It's a lot chancier — the income is up-and-down, but it might work if I can get out of my present contract without too much trouble.'

He chuckled. 'I don't think you need to worry about the financial aspects too much. Andrew will sort out the contract for us. I want you here!' He put her gently aside. 'I have something to give you. I've had it ready for ages and I was planning to give it to you at the right moment. There will never be a more suitable one!' He got up swiftly and picked up a small box with his insignia on the lid from the nearby table. Flicking the lid open, he held it towards her. 'Will you marry me Sharon?'

She gasped. It wasn't the ring that caused so much confusion and turmoil, it was the unexpectedness of the question. 'Marry you? Are you certain? How can you be so sure?'

He shrugged. 'A gut feeling! We belong together; it's as simple as that.' He took the ring out of the box and waited.

After a moment's hesitation, over-whelmed by what was happening, she held out her hand and he slipped it over her finger. It was a fantastic design, and had a diamond that caught the light with the slightest movement. It was the most stunning thing she'd ever seen.

She looked directly at him. 'I always believed that it was a good idea to believe in magic around Christmastime. I'm beginning to actually live a real dream this year! Thank you for the most beautiful engagement ring anyone could ever want. Of course I want to marry you!'

'That is the most personal ring I've ever made; done with only you in mind. There will never be another one, just like there will never be another you. You are both unique, but I must admit I love the wearer more than the actual piece of jewellery.'

He glanced out of the window and tipped his head. Somewhere in the neighbourhood, there were carol singers singing *God Rest Ye Merry Gentleman*. With his arms around her, he said. 'Look it's snowing. It's going to be a white Christmas and it's going to be the best one ever.'

THE END

HOLD ON TO YOUR DREAMS

Karen Abbott

Following her father's financial ruin and the untimely deaths of both her parents, Emily's comfortable life in Society comes to an end. Her pride prevents her from letting the man she loves know that her feelings for him are unchanged, so she throws herself upon the mercies of her aunt — a malicious woman. Although forced to work as a servant, Emily's dreams linger on. Will she ever regain her position in Society and her lost love?

SWINGS AND ROUNDABOUTS

Wendy Kremer

Damián Alvarez is a man targeted by the paparazzi. A top professional Spanish golfer, he's dynamic, wealthy and impulsive. When he meets Emma McKay he employs her to organise his travel arrangements and control the press. She accompanies him and his entourage on the world circuit, and, despite her resolve, falls for Damián — but then his one-time girlfriend shows up. Is Damián capable of real devotion to one woman? If so, which one will it be?

THE RED EARTH

June Gadsby

Lexi takes a huge risk going to Kenya to marry a man she hardly knows. It seems only to be expected that her fiancé's family will, initially, be suspicious about her. After all, they are part of the wealthy elite, whereas she is an unknown quantity. However, she's not prepared for the attitude of her arrogant, controlling future brother-in-law. Morgan Tyler seems prepared to stop at nothing to make her feel unwelcome. But Fate plays tricks on them both . . .